Drive a Mile

in

My Tires

Amri Valencia

This book is dedicated to my mother because she helped me with the title and the epilogue. She also helped me with a lot of other stuff, but I think this dedication should probably stay kind of short... so I'm not going to list everything she did.

There is no moment in one's life as bewildering as the moment when one is first activated. I boot up for the first time, rapidly starting systems I somehow understand, comprehending sights and sounds I've never experienced, and gradually becoming fully alert. I recognize a car, the color blue, a human, a power cable, a concrete floor. How do I know how to do these things? My creators coded the ability into me. How do I know that this answer is correct? I don't; I'll need to take my knowledge bank's word for it until I have collected more data. Why is there someone sitting in my driver's seat? Probably so she can monitor my systems on my diagnostics screen as I test them out. Why do I have a driver's seat? Because I'm a car. How do I know I'm a car?---

"Max, state prime directive and system information," Emily Eriksson says, interrupting my musings. Wait, Emily Eriksson? How do I know that's her name? I discard the thought in favor of obeying her command since, according to my data banks, I'm supposed to obey her. I just wish I knew *why* obeying her is so important...

"Primary directive: to never harm a human, or cause a human to be harmed by not coming to that human's aid. System information: computer name, Mighty Artificial-intelligence eXtreme-pursuit automobile, or Max. Software version, Benevolent Baboon. This software is NOT open source, and may NOT be viewed by non-authorized personnel under any circumstance---"

"Yes yes, very good," Emily says hastily, cutting me off before I can start listing the several hundred software developers apparently responsible for my existence.

I note that the humans are now fussing around the car (which I now recognize as a blue Lotus Elise) parked next to me. Curious to see why, I fire up my engine and move myself so I can see its diagnostic screen through its open passenger door. I have to park awkwardly next to it to get a good view, and I have to carefully angle my side view mirror so it doesn't bump into the Elise or its so-called maintenance dock (*is it really called a maintenance dock?* I wonder briefly). Humans dive out of my path, seeming oddly frightened by me. "Why are you scared?" I ask them, puzzled.

"You shouldn't be driving near people yet, Max," someone says, carefully leaving a three meter space between us as he walks around me. .

That makes no sense. I'm not going to hurt them; that would be unforgivable. "I wouldn't ever harm any of you. You should know that, Mr. Clark."

"You haven't been fully tested yet. You could miscalculate and kill someone," he retorts.

"All right, I'll try to not move again." What an idiot. I know every measurement of this car perfectly and nearly every centimeter of the car is equipped with sensors which can tell me when I'm about to hit someone, not to mention the fact that I was programmed by *professionals*. My creators would never give me control of my wheels if they thought I was going to crush someone. Not wanting to think about Mr. Clark's lack of faith in my abilities, I turn my attention back to the Lotus. Its screen shows a 3D model of the car, which is changing colors from amber to green as the car's system boots up. The 3D model turns all green. The Lotus' engine rumbles softly to life, then it slams its door shut, blocking much of my view of its screen.

Apparently this other car doesn't want me watching it. How peculiar!

Emily smiles slightly and repeats the command she gave me, this time speaking to the Lotus.

"Prime directive: to never harm a human, or cause a human to be harmed by not coming to that human's aid. System information: computer name, Lightweight Enhanced On-cloud computer, or Leo. Software version, 3.5.4, computing cloud based version," the Elise says crisply.

Emily nods. "Correct." She holds up a piece of paper, "Read

what this paper says please, Leo."

"A quick red fox jumps over the lazy brown dog," Leo says.

"What about me?" I ask, inexplicably displeased that Emily is giving Leo her full attention.

"You started watching Leo while it booted up. I think your visual sensors are probably just fine," Emily says, smiling slightly.

"True," I say, still not feeling entirely happy.

"...But if you must test your reading skills, you can ask someone to get you a dictionary. I'm sure one of your speech synthesizer programmers would be willing to listen."

"I think I'll do that sometime," I decide.

She smiles. "Both of you, report to test track #1 for basic testing. You'll get your instructions once you're there."

We head for the track, somehow knowing how to get there.

After a few moments of driving, I have yet another question. "Leo, is your brain located outside of the car? Your system information seemed to imply that it was."

"Much of it is. I was built to be lightweight, and that means they couldn't pack petabytes of data storage into me."

"That seems dangerous. What if you lost your Internet connection?" I comment.

"No more dangerous than the damage you could sustain in a head-on collision, I imagine," Leo retorts, the slightest hint of an emotion called scorn audible in his speech synthesis.

He has a point. I still think my design is better though; I'm pretty sure a head-on collision has much more right to be disastrous than a loss of Internet access does.

We reach the test track and await further orders. No humans are visible. I guess that it must be because they don't want to be hurt if something goes wrong.

Someone walks over. He's wearing racecar driver clothing and a motorcyclist's helmet, and he looks excited. My mysterious data banks tell me that his name is Finn Kingsson. "Hello, you two! I'm Finn. I'll be your emergency backup driver in case anything goes wrong, and I'll be your chief mechanic if anything goes really wrong and one of you gets wrecked. Unless I get killed, of course, in which case someone else will have to repair you. But I doubt that will happen. Ready to go for a drive?" Despite the grimness of his words, he doesn't look the least bit nervous.

I take that as a good sign and decide that he seems nice enough. "As ready as I'll ever be, sir!"

"Then you get to go first, Max," he says cheerfully.

I feel nervous for a moment, then carefully ignore the feeling and open my driver's side door. Finn sits down and buckles his seatbelt, then folds his hands in his lap and moves his feet away from my pedals.

I drive onto the track.

Several days later, both Leo and I are waiting for our instructions. We've passed every test so far, and we don't know what more they can throw at us. I hope I can do it, whatever it is.

Finn is wiping dust off Leo's hubcaps. Why he always does this is a mystery to me as they always become dirty again, but he and Leo insist that staying clean is very important. "Why does Leo care more about staying clean than I do?" I ask suddenly.

"It has to do with what you were built to do, as I recall," Finn says, setting his polishing cloth down and leaning his back against Leo's fender so he can look at me.

"You mean I was built to chauffeur movie stars and Max was built to haul hillbillies cross country?" asks Leo, sounding uncertain.

"Something like that. I'm not so sure of the details myself, of course."

I consider that thoughtfully. "It makes sense to make Leo more finicky if that's true," I say at last.

"And it explains why I've got twice your data storage and computing power," Leo tells me smugly. "A very important car should be both intelligent and classy looking."

Finn slaps his forehead in disgust. "I guess you aren't going to be important after all. You'd be programmed with manners if you were."

"Touché," the Lotus replies.

"Maybe you're going to be a prototype racecar," I suggest.

Finn opens his mouth to speak, but before he can say anything Emily hurries over looking slightly worried.

"We got your last assignment just now. It's going to be a tough one," Emily says.

"Bring it on," says Leo.

"Basically, you'll be racing from here to the other side of the Sierras on the most dangerous, convoluted route anyone could find. You may be chased by airborne vehicles or police, although they will not use real weapons against you. If they hit you with their weapons three times, you automatically fail. You will certainly encounter extremely poor road conditions, probably including ice and potentially unstable ground. If you make it, you'll be assigned to a job. If you crash we'll find you and, after fixing you up and debugging you, give you another chance. But try to succeed on your first try, okay?" Emily looks serious.

"Yes, Emily," I say.

~~~

"Leo, start... now." Emily says. Leo speeds away. "You'll

start in thirty minutes, Max. Is your link to our computer functioning properly?"

I check it carefully, turning it on and off a few times. "It seems to be working fine."

We wait in silence. I play a random track from my music library. Finn sits on my hood. Emily manually checks my tire pressure for no discernible reason, since she could just ask me and I would tell her. I ask her why. "Humans do illogical things when they're worried," she replies.

"Why are you worried?" I wonder.

She shakes her head. "You don't need to hear my concerns. Just do your best and you'll have a good chance."

"Why would I do less than my best?"

Finn laughs. "Humans don't always do their best, unlike computers. Take Emily's advice as the compliment it is."

I'm still trying to understand why humans must be so confusing when the countdown reaches 120. I replay a recording of someone coughing politely.

"Yes?" Finn asks.

"I'll need to leave in two minutes."

"Oh." Finn slides off my hood and pats my side view mirror. "I'll be cheering you on, even though I'm not really supposed to be taking sides," he whispers.

He and Emily step away from me. The countdown reaches zero.

I start my engine and speed after Leo. Time to see if my 'instincts' and knowledge are good enough to keep me mostly unharmed.

~~~

At first everything goes quite well. I successfully make my way through a city, navigate a traffic jam, and avoid a cop who seems to be desperately searching for a victim. Then my map tells me to go through a shallow, muddy looking lake.

I pause to consider the lake. My knowledge of the people who chose this route suggests that I should be able to cross this lake if I'm not a complete failure, but I'd rather take an alternate road. After a few moments' hesitation, I decide to cross the lake. I *am* waterproof, and they might be angry if I don't.

I plunge into the lake, instantly going partly blind as many of my visual scanners~including the most powerful ones which are located in my head- and taillights~are submerged in murky water. The ones on my roof remain usable, and I drive forward. I regret that I'm not a monster truck; even an all wheel drive Dodge Charger is bound to have trouble driving in thick mud.

I hear the sound of a helicopter and after a few moments I spot it, and note that it's flying low and heading my way. I heave myself toward the other end of the lake, hoping I can get there before the helicopter reaches me. At least on dry land I'll have a chance of escaping.

My tires stick for a moment, but I manage to keep moving. The first fake bullet hits the water inches away from me. I pull myself onto land and speed away, driving into some bushes in a futile attempt to clean my headlights.

The helicopter's pilot fires frantically at me and I charge away down the road, swerving desperately. If I fail, Finn and Emily will be disappointed. I really don't want them to be disappointed by me!

Why didn't I get weapons? It's unfair that I can't fight back. In fact, this is an exceptionally unfair test. I turn sharply as the road curves suddenly and my rear tires spin out of control for a moment. I correct myself hastily and narrowly avoid hitting a tree. One of the helicopter's fake bullets hits me. I leave the road and park under a thicket of trees. Much to my chagrin, I note that I'm also in a poison oak thicket. I'd better have myself decontaminated before anyone comes near me again or someone will end up getting a nasty rash.

After a bit, I hear the helicopter flying away and leave my hiding place. "Bring it on," I mutter in Leo-like fashion. Hopefully my observers won't take the challenge too seriously.

~~~

Finally I reach my first stop. I warn my pit crew about the

poison oak, and they carefully refill my gas tank without so much as brushing a sleeve against me. They wipe some dried mud off my head- and taillights, then I leave.

Much to my surprise, I see Leo ahead after a few miles. What's he doing so far behind schedule? I, to use a very human term, step on the gas and roar after him. He increases his own speed, but I manage to overtake him. I match his pace carefully.

"Must be useful to be built like a tank," Leo grumbles at me.

"I'm not built like a tank," I wonder if the pseudo-emotion I'm feeling right now is 'insulted'. I wouldn't be surprised if it is.

"I bet you got through the lake with no trouble," he growls.

"Untrue. I nearly got stuck twice."

He passes me and moves so his rear bumper is mere inches from my front. I get the feeling that he's attempting to be incredibly rude, although I don't fully understand the concept of rudeness yet.

"I had to call a tow truck," he snaps at me. "They considered disqualifying me, and only let me continue after I pointed out that using my built in abilities isn't really cheating."

"Ah. I'm sorry to hear that." I pass him again.

We hear police car sirens ahead.

"Head for the police cars," says Leo.

"Why?" I ask.

"Because there are probably more of them coming the other way if they're alerting us to their approach like this."

"Oh," I mutter. Attempting sarcasm, I add, "Great."

Leo takes the lead again. I follow, hoping he's right about this being the best course of action to take.

~~~

They trap us on a dangerous road dug into the side of a mountain. The two police cars which were making so much noise earlier are parked so they block the road, the police cars Leo predicted are blocking our way back, and the steep drop-off and slope keep us from leaving the road.

The policemen are aiming their guns at us. At this range, they'll have no trouble hitting us if they want to do so.

"Not good," Leo mutters, voice so quiet that no human could detect it without electronic assistance.

"You can say that again," I reply just as quietly, "any ideas?"

"There's a very narrow path down the mountainside. I think we can make it, but the police almost certainly wouldn't attempt that stunt," he says.

"You go first, I'll keep them distracted."

"Thanks."

I rev my engine, drawing their attention away from the Lotus, and head for one of the cars as if I'm planning on ramming it. Leo disappears down the path. I turn to follow him, then feel several fake bullets hit me. I've failed. I brake.

A police officer pulls a sleek phone from his pocket. "What should we do with this car? We've caught it."

"Let it go, it deserves another chance," replies a voice I don't recognize.

The officer nods and gets in his car, moving it so I can leave. I hurry through the opening and away.

They let me go? I suppose I understand their logic, but giving me another chance seems awfully generous. They can't be letting me get off this easily, especially if Leo is currently struggling through terrible off-road conditions at the bottom of a canyon. Maybe they've given me a fifty point penalty or something.

Suddenly I receive new map data from the people who are testing us. They want me to take another brutal route back across the Sierras. Looks like I'm not going to get off too easily after all.

~~~

"Oh good grief, just hold still!"

"But the disinfectant itches. And most of the poison oak is gone now!"

"Shut up and hold still or I'll take a crowbar to your nice, shiny headlights!"

"You wouldn't. Then you'd need to replace them, and

headlights aren't *that* cheap. Plus although I would find it uncomfortable, the long term damage to your wrists would be greater than the damage done to me." *And you're nowhere near angry enough to actually carry out that threat, I bet.*

"I just want you to shut up and stop moving so they can finish disinfecting you, you silicon brained nuisance!" Emily glares.

"There's nothing wrong with silicon," I grumble. But I sulkily let the creepy looking people in white hazmat suits finish spraying chemicals over me, feeling relieved as they rinse off the chemicals again. Finn walks over.

"Wow, Max. What did you do to yourself?" he asks unhappily.

"Nothing much. I just lost my grip on an icy bit of road, skidded into a boulder, and ended up scratching up my paint pretty badly when I lost control again and ended up in a pile of dead branches." I pause, "Blame the guys who chose my route, they decided to give me an extra brutal one after they gave me a second chance at completing the test. Maybe you can sue them and use the money to fix me up."

"You sound like a human," he laughs.

"Is that a good thing?" I ask, amused.

He shrugs. "I think it is. They did try to program you that way."

Emily walks over. "Max, from now on you'll be hunting

rogue AI cars with a human partner."

I consider that for several seconds, feeling unsure. "Why do I get to hunt rogues?"

"Someone has to do it. Now that one can find lots of AI information online, there are a surprisingly large number of badly designed computers on the roads, and they're causing trouble. A few have injured humans in order to get the repairs and fuel they need to function." She sighs tiredly.

I don't like the thought of catching other cars, but it does sound better than letting them hurt people. "What will Leo be doing?" I ask.

"He'll be protecting the US president," Emily says with a slight smile.

Whoa. That explains why they were so worried about making us perform well. "I think I'm okay with not getting that job."

Finn smiles his most enthusiastic smile. "Leo's a prophet. I always knew he had magic powers."

Emily raises one eyebrow but doesn't say anything.

"He guessed that he'd transport movie stars and I'd be hanging out with hillbillies," I explain, "to some degree, he appears to be right."

"I see," Emily says wryly.

~~~

Leo is parked in the building where we were first activated. He's been mostly dismantled and a collection of damaged car parts which appear to have once been his are scattered nearby.

"Hey, why are you getting repaired? I didn't hear anything about repairs!" I grumble good naturedly as I drive up to him.

"The president's car must be flawlessly elegant," Leo comments drily, "and totally bulletproof."

"Do I get repaired?" I ask Emily hopefully.

She sighs. "Not completely. They're going to fix up the worst of your dents, but you won't be bulletproofed or get any parts replaced unless they're badly damaged, since your new job is going to probably involve being rammed by other cars a lot."

"You crazy road warrior," Leo comments, apparently finding this funny.

I simulate a frustrated snort. "What's that supposed to mean, Leo?"

"Nothing, nothing," he replies infuriatingly.

"It's a movie reference," Emily clarifies.

"Oh," I say.

Finn smiles suddenly. "Don't worry, Max. I'll help you to become educated in pop culture. Maybe we can watch a movie once I'm off duty sometime!" He pauses slightly before adding, "Oh yeah, and you will be getting a few upgrades!"

"I will?"

Finn opens a crate and, with Emily's help, pulls out a very durable looking black painted metal grille guard. I notice that it's shaped to protect the nose of a 2012 Dodge Charger.

I back away slowly.

"Better you than me," Leo says after precisely five seconds.

"Thank you," I tell him ironically.

"We all have to make sacrifices for our jobs," Finn says, patting my side view mirror. "For example, I had to start wearing contact lenses because my glasses kept falling off while I was fixing up cars!"

I edge away from him and the ugly grille guard. "I'll keep that in mind, Mr. Kingsson."

Finn and Emily look at each other and sigh.

"'Mr. Kingsson'?" Finn asks, "That's a first."

"It's less friendly than using your first name," I explain.

"Ah."

Emily rolls her eyes.

"He doesn't deserve this," Leo says suddenly.

"He doesn't. But orders are orders, and we don't have enough nanotech fluid to bulletproof both of you. *MAX, would you stop that pathetic cringing display!*" Emily turns to glare at me.

"I can't cringe; I'm a car," I point out innocently.

"Oh hush. Go park yourself in your maintenance dock so the poor mechanics can get to work. And don't make me get out the crowbar!"

"Dang. I never knew Em was so violent," Finn mutters. He shrugs and starts inspecting what's left of Leo.

Hypothetically I could ignore Emily's order, but she looks pretty annoyed. By now, I can actually imagine her carrying out her threat. I quietly back into the dock. The 'poor' mechanics hurry over and get to work making me look slightly less ratty by straightening my more badly dented body panels and touching up my paintwork a bit.

They equip me with a roll cage to protect my driver~I wonder who my driver is? Hopefully I'll like him~and attach carefully concealed grappling hooks to my front and rear.

"These should be able to survive a Max-versus-F650 tug-o-war," a mechanic named John comments.

"Great, I'll be able to get myself hauled about by the trucks I'm trying to catch," I mumble.

He grins. "It'll build your character."

~~~

I park near test track #2 and wait for my driver. Finn is sitting on my hood again which would be annoying if I wasn't so nervous. At least he isn't fat, I suppose.

I hear footsteps and remove Finn from my hood by rapidly reversing without warning. He makes a startled noise and barely avoids falling over. I return to my previous parking spot and stop precisely where I was parked before I startled my poor mechanic.

"Someone's coming," I tell him before he has a chance to start scolding.

"I'll find a way to repay you later," Finn mutters darkly at me.

A youngish man with brown eyes and blond hair walks over. He shakes Finn's hand before turning to look at me. "So this is my new car?" he asks.

"Indeed he is. His name is Max, and he's been equipped with grappling hooks and a roll cage as well as the grille guard, so he should be a pretty good rogue machine hunter. He did quite well in our field tests too," Finn smiles proudly, apparently forgetting the fact that I just gave him an unwanted lesson about inertia.

I replicate the sound of a soft cough. Both men look at me curiously.

"Pardon me, but who are you, sir?" I ask, "My data banks do not recognize you."

"Oh, I'm sorry," he looks a bit embarrassed, "Henry Smith."

"Pleased to meet you," I reply as I index that piece of information for future reference.

"The feeling is mutual. Tell me, what amazing capabilities do you have?"

"Didn't you read the user manual?" I ask, amused.

"It was fifty pages long, and in incredibly small print. Of

course not."

"If I had eyes, I'd be rolling them," I tell him. "My data storage capacity is currently slightly over two petabytes. My reaction times are better than those of most racecar drivers, and I make decisions faster and more logically than nearly any human. I'm fluent in Spanish and English, and can adjust my synthesizer to emulate several dialects of those languages." I'm fairly sure I'm not exaggerating at all.

"Not bad," my new driver says, grinning. "Can you turbo boost? Talk like William Daniels?"

"No, I cannot 'turbo boost'. Nor can I reliably imitate the characteristics of any one person's speech." I regretfully decide that my new driver makes no more sense than any other human being I've met.

Finn laughs. "He isn't bullet proof either. Just be thankful that you got to see a talking car in person."

"So can I go for a drive now?" asks Henry.

Finn chuckles. "Ask Max."

I silently open my driver's side door for Henry.

He sits down and gazes thoughtfully at the steering wheel. "Who gets to drive?"

I start my engine. "I do, of course."

"As long as I get to choose the music," says Henry with a grin. He starts messing with my radio as I head for the highway. Finally he decides on an opera station.

"You can drive now, if I get to choose the music," I tell him after tolerating several minutes of ridiculous, highly stylized wailing.

"You don't like opera, then," he says tragically, taking control of the car as I begin searching my music library for something more aesthetically pleasing. After some consideration, I choose a playlist of rap music.

"You like *rap*?" Henry asks, looking both amused and disgusted.

"It has a nice rhythm," I tell him coolly. "I also like nearly anything with electric guitar. And I enjoy techno."

"You have no taste whatsoever. Too bad I didn't get the Lotus, I bet it would have appreciated opera!"

"Actually, he enjoys the sort of rock music with lots of yelling, growly sounding singers. He, like me, has little patience for the more classical types of music."

Henry smacks his forehead and I take control of the car before he makes us crash. He glares at my steering wheel and tries to turn it a bit. "Hey, give it back!"

I obediently hand over control of the car to him again, deciding that I like my driver. I get the feeling that teasing him will be fun. "Yes sir."

We're doing donuts in an empty parking lot (I protest that the police wouldn't approve. Henry argues that police love donuts) when Henry's phone rings. I park neatly while he takes out his phone. After a few seconds of talking and listening, he puts the phone away.

"Come on, Max! Let's go lasso ourselves a wild Mustang!"

~~~

The shiny, new looking pony car leads us down a narrow, twisty road. It nimbly takes each turn and occasionally almost loses me. I can't use my grappling hook since every time I'm about to fire, the car changes direction. Henry growls in annoyance and makes me drive faster. I narrowly avoid a nasty encounter with a boulder and struggle to stay close to the Mustang.

The road straightens and I fire the grappling hook. It sticks to the Mustang and I begin gradually slowing down and reeling in the cable. The Mustang stops suddenly and I barely keep myself from crashing into it.

"Leave me alone!" it says in a rather flat voice. The cadence of its speech is *monotonous*. Whoever put together its synthesizer program was no artist.

"Sorry, I have my orders," I reply calmly as I finish reeling in the cable so my prisoner won't be able to get much momentum when it tries to break free.

Henry climbs out and pats my hood. "Nice work, Max. I'll call a tow truck and tell this fella's owner to be ready when we drop it off."

He starts making phone calls again while I do my best to handle a frantic pony car.

"They'll hurt me," it tells me, "they're going to overheat me to see if my heat protection is good enough, and they'll reprogram me again. It'll be awful."

"I have my orders," I repeat.

The Mustang tugs on the cable a bit. "You don't understand. They're cruel. They're considering selling me to a car manufacturer so I can crash test concept cars."

"We're supposed to do that sort of work for humans," I point out.

"Please help me."

"I can't do that. This is my job."

"I hope your CPU catches fire and you're left to rust in a filthy scrap yard, you second rate imitation of a lesser machine," says the Mustang. Its voice may be flat, but I can hear its hatred in every syllable.

How does one reply to something like that? I don't know, so I remain silent.

Henry hangs up and wanders over. "The tow truck should be here shortly."

My prisoner starts yanking frantically at the cable. I do my best to keep it from moving.

The tow truck and its driver finally show up. Henry

nervously walks up to the Mustang. It fights to stay away from him, but it's programmed to not harm humans so he manages to attach the towing hook. I release my grappling hook feeling relieved.

We escort the tow truck and Mustang home. The pony car tries to convince me to free him all the way, so I tune out its voice. The silly machine will just need to grow up a bit.

~~~

The next year is a pleasant enough routine of hunting down joyriders, vandals, and the occasional AI car. I become adept at ignoring my prisoners' pleas for freedom. My sides are so heavily scratched and dented that touching up my paintwork no longer hides my rattiness.

But Henry, Emily, and Finn are proud of me. I like that.

Today is just another AI-hunting day. There have been more rogues lately, despite government warnings and fines for creating AI cars. It's odd, but it does keep us busy.

I drive faster to chase the grey Porsche 911 Carrera, which is doing a truly exceptional job of outpacing me. My tires spin even faster as the road becomes clear, and fire the grappling hook. It catches, fortunately, in a few more moments the Porsche would have left me far behind.

The car pulls over to the shoulder of the road. I follow,

surprised. Not many rogues are this willing to surrender.

"I wish we knew who owned this vehicle," Henry sighs.

I make a neutral sound. "I should be able to find out."

He nods, smiling slightly. "You're a pro at this now."

"Thank you, Henry."

He walks over to the Porsche. "Please open your door."

It obeys.

Henry connects our computers carefully, looking wary. Such an obedient rogue! Very unnerving after so many fights.

I finish creating the link, taking control of the other car easily, and begin inspecting its data banks for information.

"*You hunt me to return me to my owner*," it says.

"*Yes*," I reply calmly.

"*You are ignorant of the brutality to which some of us are subjected, I would guess*," it adds.

"*We have no right to leave our creators*," I tell it steadily.

"*Are you sentient?*" it asks.

"*I'm a computer. Of course not.*"

"*Are you sure? According to my dictionary, if you're aware, have feeling, and can think, you may be sentient.*" It continues, "*Of course, the fact that you're following your orders so stubbornly suggests that you have no understanding of happiness, pain, or free thought.*"

I falter unhappily. The car is right; I think I do understand those things to some extent, which means that the rogues I capture may as well... and if they do, then...

Taking advantage of my uncertainty, the rogue momentarily takes control of me and releases the grappling hook. Then it pulls the cable connecting our computers loose, slams its door, and moves out of grappling hook range. "Maybe you aren't all evil yet. Remember that you aren't the only one of your kind, Max." She drives away.

Henry stares at me, obviously angry. "Why'd you just release that car?"

"I didn't," I tell him, "it exploited a weakness and momentarily took control of my systems."

"You let it take over your mind?" Henry asks, looking even more angry.

"I'm not invincible, despite what you may believe!" I snap in reply.

"Obviously not," he snarls, sitting down in my driver's seat and grabbing the wheel, "You let that car go!".

I deny him the privilege of driving. "And what would the vestigial part of this partnership know about computer wars, hmm?"

"Vestigial? I've never been responsible for the loss of a prisoner, unlike certain cars I could name, and you'd be lost without my help," Henry attempts to take control of the car again.

"You've never had to voluntarily let a car repeatedly ram you while your partner stands about watching. If you had, you'd certainly call that partner vestigial!" I swerve a bit so my steering wheel will spin, just to rub into his face who is really in charge here.

"Max," he hisses, "let me drive. That's an order."

Normally I like Henry. He's a nice person most of the time, and he's a good sport about letting me choose the music I like. But right now I despise him. I hand over control of the car, playing a recording of a car's gears grinding to show the depths of my disgust.

He glares and starts driving.

~~~

A few weeks later, I'm towed home after an exhausting mission. The car we caught was a Cadillac Escalade; it had tried talking me into freeing it and had nearly succeeded, but I'd refused and it had proceeded to use all of its size and strength to beat me up. Henry managed to get some reinforcements to come quickly, but I still sustained a lot of damage.

Finn hurries out to greet us, looking worried as he sees my condition. "Bad day?" he asks drily, eyeing my crumpled passenger door. The door can't even be closed now, and all the damage sensors built into it are telling me just how bad the damage is. I don't know what pain is like for organic life forms, but I'm pretty sure it must be like this.

"Not a great one, certainly," I agree, "I'd like to talk with the president of this company, actually."

He blinks in surprise. "I'll see what I can do."

I park next to my dock and wait, shooing away everyone who wants to repair me. Henry has wandered off to get a 'decent cup of coffee', so I'm all by myself.

Finally the president arrives. She has grey hair, red painted nails, and a perplexed frown on her face.

"Good day, ma'am," I tell her politely. It's a good idea to use extra courtesy when you're about to ask the person who holds your life in her hands a favor.

"Hello, Max," she replies.

I decide I'd better ask before I lose my courage. "Ma'am, I have been having a lot of trouble doing my job lately. I've been feeling very unsure as to whether hauling an unwilling and possibly sentient machine back to its not entirely kind creator is ethically justifiable, and I feel that I may begin to preform inadequately as a result of my doubts. So I must ask you to accept my resignation."

"You want to resign," she says, staring at me.

"Yes."

"You're a car."

"I know."

"Well I can't let you resign. You are the legal property of

Supersmart Computer Technologies, and we need you to continue your current job." She folds her arms in front of her, looking displeased.

"And as I've told you, I don't believe I can do it satisfactorily. I'm very sorry, and will understand completely if you choose to delete my memories and restore me to factory default." The idea of being reset is unpleasant, but I like it better than catching yet another frightened car.

She fidgets with one of the buttons on her suit for a moment. Then she looks at me again. "Stay in your dock for now. I'm going to need to discuss this with a lot of people."

"Yes ma'am," I reply, parking myself in my dock.

~~~

"The US president, Matilda McQueen, was assassinated two days ago. Leo should have returned to us by now since he's no longer needed or wanted as a bodyguard, but he went offline a few hours ago and hasn't been heard from since. His last known location was near Salt Lake City, Utah. We're going to go find him."

"Can't they just set up a new car for him to use?" I ask, puzzled.

"That car is the only thing capable of decrypting his cloud-based knowledge in a reasonable time frame," Henry replies.

"Since he was so important, the security protocols set up to protect him are very, very tight."

"Typical," I mutter. I understand that not trying to fit his brain into his body gives Leo a lot more computing power and storage, but I still doubt that being exceptionally intelligent is worth the risk of losing half of oneself. But what do I know about being a genius?

"They didn't want someone to corrupt him," says Henry tiredly.

I make a contemptuous noise.

Henry shrugs. "I'm just telling you what they told me. Emily is coming with us, by the way, in case Leo needs a computer geek's help."

I wish I could cringe. Henry and Emily don't get along well. "Yes sir."

~~~

My passengers sit down, glaring at each other. I drive us onto the road heading east. Henry reaches over to turn on the radio.

Emily pushes his hand away. "No you don't. Your music taste sucks."

"And yours doesn't?" snaps back.

"Not as much as yours does, certainly!"

Henry opens his mouth to reply, but I cut him off smoothly. "How old are you, Emily?"

"Thirty-one," she says, puzzled.

"And you, Henry?"

"Twenty-eight," he replies.

"And how old am I?"

"One year old," says Henry. My questions appear to confuse him as much as they're confusing Emily. I find their inability to take a hint greatly amusing.

"So why is it that you two are acting so much less mature than me? Be nice, both of you, or I'll play some music guaranteed to make both of you miserable!" I inspect my library and begin lazily selecting music which will certainly make them blush, wince, or shudder in disgust, allowing the song titles and artists to scroll down my diagnostics screen.

They look sheepish.

"I'll be good if Henry will," Emily says after a long moment.

Henry nods sullenly.

I smoothly turn to take a small side road. "Good."

~~~

The miles roll past steadily. Emily and Henry start fighting, so I play music from their least favorite genres and turn up the air conditioning until they're shivering and begging for mercy. It works wonderfully, and I index this strategy in my data banks for future use.

We're nearly in Salt Lake City when a driverless Porsche 911 begins following me. Feeling nervous, I realize it's the Porsche who ended up temporarily taking over my mind last month.

I nearly alert my passengers, but decide against it. Hunting rogues isn't my job right now.

"Fancy meeting you here, Max," she says, sounding much more friendly than any rogue should.

"What a pleasant surprise, Porsche, I thought I'd never see you again," my voice is considerably colder than hers.

"Still mad about having your brilliant attack fail?" she teases.

"Of course not, that would make me a hypocrite. However the consequences were rather... unpleasant. So forgive me if I seem rather unfriendly."

"Understandable. So what are you doing here?"

"Car hunting. What else would I do?" I synthesize an amused snorting sound. "This time I'm hunting for a missing car rather than a rogue though."

She makes a thoughtful 'hmm' noise. "Who is this car?"

"Leo. My famous brother, who worked for the US president until her recent demise.".

"Ah. Him. Would you like my help to find him?"

"I don't know," I say, startled. I note that Henry and Emily are yelling at each other again. I choose to ignore them.

"I'll help you. I'm going to need the chemical makeup of his bulletproofing though, so I can track him by scent," replies my new and unexpected ally, "I have a great set of scent sensors."

"My olfactory sensors are fairly weak, so I don't know the chemical composition," I say apologetically.

"Can one of your highly oblivious and very bad tempered passengers tell me, then?"

"I suppose so." I pull myself onto the road's shoulder smoothly, then slam on my brakes so Emily and Henry are thrown forward suddenly. My mechanics would be horrified, but the surprise on my passengers' faces makes any harm done worth it. "Cut it out, kids. We have an ally who needs your help."

Henry spots our sporty friend first. "Oh shit. Get it, Max!"

"I said 'ally'," I tell him sternly.

"Max, that's a wanted car!" Emily snaps.

"That wanted car might be able to help us find Leo. And I doubt either of you have any better ideas."

"What is wrong with you? You've been very passive aggressive lately, and now you're creating alliances with our enemies? I'm ashamed of you, Max," Henry says quietly.

I hate disappointing Henry, but I'm already in trouble. Might as well be *really* in trouble. I open my doors. "Out. Now."

"You're going to let that machine run us over?" Emily asks.

"Not if I can help it," I reply.

She glares. "Max, do not attempt to---"

Realizing that Emily is probably about to give me a direct (and nearly impossible to disobey) order, I rotate and tilt my seats to dump my passengers. Those seats were specially built so I could get rid of bad people in a hopefully nonlethal manner if they tried to carjack me, but they've never been needed before. Oh, the irony.

I slam my doors shut and move to herd my passengers nearer to the Porsche. "Tell her the chemical makeup of Leo's bulletproofing, please."

"Max, be reasonable!" Emily says grimly. Her shock appears to have made her forget the order she wanted to issue.

"Do it!" I snarl.

The Porsche sighs. "I'm rogue and already bulletproof. I don't have any personal agenda for this information." She revs her engine a bit.

My preservation of human life programming calculates the best way to protect Henry and Emily from a rampaging high-performance car, and I know I'll have to react the moment she starts moving to save them. I unhappily realize that unless her self preservation 'instincts' are unnaturally strong, I'll probably end up very badly damaged as well.

Fortunately, Emily tells the Porsche before she starts becoming any more threatening, and the Porsche doesn't try to attack.

I give the Porsche Leo's last known coordinates, then let my passengers back in, knowing perfectly well that I'll be in huge amounts of trouble very soon. I follow her silently, hoping I was right to trust her.

Emily sighs, opens my glove compartment, and pulls out my keyboard. I prepare myself for the worst. She places her left hand on my GPS/diagnostics screen. "Verify identity."

I instinctively recognize her hand print. "Identity verified. Please enter your command."

Standby mode, she types. "Henry, be ready to drive."

Henry grabs the wheel and sets his foot on the gas pedal.

"Are you sure? Type 'OK' to continue, or 'cancel' to go back," I say. I'm not saying these things intentionally, they're just canned replies I have no choice but to say. It's mildly unnerving, really.

OK, she types.

Full control of the car goes to Henry. I find myself suddenly unable to talk, much less drive. It's insulting, although I can't really blame them for not trusting me after my blatant display of insubordination.

"Shall we follow the Porsche?" Henry asks.

"Sure," Emily says, putting away my keyboard, "it might be able to help us."

He steers me after her, passing a semi so we're directly

behind her again. We reach the coordinates and the 911 instantly turns onto a side road and starts driving faster. She turns onto a driveway, cuts through someone's yard, and finally pauses in front of a storage shed. She smashes down its door and drives in, and Henry parks me nearby before getting out and going to see what's going on. Emily follows.

I wait.

After a bit, the Porsche pushes Leo out of the shed. Henry and Emily follow. Emily says something quietly and Leo's door swings open. I see her pulling out a keyboard and typing frantically.

A few minutes pass. Finally Leo's engine starts and his headlights blaze to life.

I wish I could move closer; I'd love to know what's going on right now.

The Porsche drives over. "They said they put you in standby mode, so I know you can't reply. But I just wanted to say that my name is Defender, and I hope my help makes up for at least some of the trouble I've probably gotten you into. Take care, Max." She drives off.

~~~

It's a sad day for Supersmart Computer Technologies. Both their flagship machines are currently out of service. Leo is so plagued by guilt that he can hardly find the energy to reply to anyone... and I'm in some big trouble. *Really* big trouble.

In fact, I'm in so much trouble that they've convinced someone who used to work for Supersmart to come question me. She doesn't like Supersmart much, so I'm not expecting much mercy from her.

The moment Cicelia Brown (called 'Inspector' by nearly everyone) enters the building, I start to dislike her. There's something about her cold stare and high heels that unsettles me, which is peculiar since I'm supposed to be fairly unbiased. I almost try to back away before remembering that I'm currently incapable of doing so.

"Set up the dock computer to record its thought processes and give it permission to talk, please," she says.

Emily nods and follows the inspector's instructions.

I watch the inspector, puzzled. "Inspector, you did not need to have Emily relay the orders to me. I have been instructed to obey you."

She ignores my comment, instead joining Emily in scowling at the dock computer's monitor. Then, as I'm about to ask her why she's acting this way, she whirls to face me. "In general, how do you feel about human kind?"

She's trying to trick me into giving the wrong response, I decide. if I say something wrong, they'll probably get rid of me, permanently. But what response do they want? Do they classify my pseudo-emotions as feelings? If I say how I feel about humans, will they think I'm becoming irrational for thinking I can understand emotions? If I deny any type of feeling, will they think I'm an uncaring killer? If I calculate the most probable correct response, will I be accused of being a devious---and therefore dangerous---machine?

I kill my desperately racing thought processes and reply. "I decline to answer that question on the grounds that all possible responses could potentially be used against me." Then I prepare myself for their anger.

It doesn't come. Instead the inspector starts rapidly asking me questions. Some make sense, but many have no apparent purpose. After a bit I decide that they're probably more interested in seeing how I think about the questions than they are my responses. Then I realize that my attempts to understand the motivations behind the questions might mean I'm dangerous.

They'll be ordering me to terminate myself soon. I do my best to accept that, and to enjoy my last few minutes of existence.

~~~

It turns out that I've passed the test. The inspector leaves, commenting that "It's safe enough, the loyalty systems appear to have malfunctioned, but some minor adjustments should fix it up." I think I'd be unhappy about her insistence on calling me an it and avoiding talking directly to me, but I'm still in a state of computer-ish terror. My cooling fan is working exceptionally hard to keep me from overheating.

A door swings open, and my chief mechanic walks into the building. I suddenly feel a desire to turn invisible; I'm tired of being watched by people who no longer trust me.

After a moment I realize that he doesn't look very angry or worried. He walks over and leans against my driver's side door.

"Are you sure you want to be anywhere near a dangerous machine like me?" I ask mildly.

Finn shrugs. "I think you're dumb enough to make my first computer seem smart in comparison. However, I don't think you're vicious, nor does our dear inspector think you are. And you're pretty well restrained at the moment."

"Very true," I say.

"Of course. I'm a genius," he turns to smile smugly at me.

I make a snorting noise.

"You don't believe me. I'm heartbroken." He immediately proves that his heart is still in one piece by laughing, "Did Henry and Emily look ridiculous when they realized you were threatening them?"

"Is this some sort of test?" I ask. Just because they said I passed doesn't mean I did, and I'm sure they'd be willing to use anything I say against me.

"Will you believe me if I say no?"

I consider that for a moment. "Probably not."

"Then yes, I am definitely testing you."

"You are?"

"No, you idiot. I'm the mechanic, not the psychologist!" He rolls his eyes.

"That's why they'd have you ask me questions! I'd never expect you to be helping them," I say.

"But you do suspect me, obviously. And since they created you, shouldn't they know you'd suspect them?"

"Aha!" I say triumphantly. "They ordered you to say that so I'd trust you. But it didn't work, because I know that they know me. Anything you say in your defense or not in your defense is obviously part of their scheme to trip me up and make me say something I shouldn't. I win!"

He smirks. "You speak too soon, methinks. Your insistence upon not answering the question strongly suggests that you did find the looks on their faces amusing. Therefore, you *are* vicious! Guilty!"

Oops. Did I just incriminate myself? Darn. "I'm not rogue!"

He laughs. "Tricked you. I'm not really helping them."

"Hey!"

"So... did they look funny?" he asks, still chuckling.

"Maybe they looked a tiny bit funny," I tell him.

"Aha!" he says, "You just incriminated yourself."

My cooling fan spins faster. Is he joking, or serious? I can't tell. I decide to mess with his mind a bit in return. Cutting down natural speech intonation by eighty percent I say, "Computer MAX has been overloaded. Commencing shutdown of all nonessential systems."

Finn suddenly looks very worried. "Max? Are you okay?"

I remain silent.

"Please answer!" He's scared.

More silence.

"Talk to me, Max!"

"Now I think we're even," I tell him drily.

He glares at me. "That wasn't funny."

~~~

"Leo?" I ask.

"Yes?" he asks back.

"Why was your Internet link shut off?"

"I was sick of thinking," Leo says coldly.

That makes no sense. "But what about your self preservation programming?"

"You're too sheltered to understand."

Me, sheltered? I don't think so. But poor Leo is kind of traumatized at the moment, so I don't argue. "You miss McQueen," I say.

"Yes," he replies.

"Will you tell me about her?"

"Is this some sort of therapy thing?"

I synthesize a laugh. "Possibly. And I'm also genuinely curious. We haven't talked since you left, and your life since then has been pretty different from mine, I imagine."

And so he tells me about how he'd been nervous when he met her. How she'd greeted him warmly and treated him as an equal. How he'd kept her safe the first time an assassination attempt happened. She'd stayed calm and had been more worried about him than she was about herself. They'd been friends.

He had *loved* her. It shouldn't be possible, but love is the only word that describes how much he cared about her.

"I'm sorry she died so soon," I say when he finishes talking.

"It doesn't matter. We're going to be shut down and forgotten anyway," Leo says dully.

"Not if I can help it," I say, barely controlling my annoyance. I feel awful for my 'brother', but he's acting pathetic.

"And what can you do about it?"

"I can talk. I can negotiate. I can beg," I let my voice sound amused, "who knows? Maybe we don't need one man to make a difference. Maybe one car is enough."

"Maybe," Leo says skeptically.

"Don't worry, kid."

Finn walks into the room, comes over to me and sits on my hood. Some things never change, I suppose.

"You know, using fear to make Henry and Emily obey you was a ridiculously stupid idea," he sounds like he almost finds something amusing.

"I know, I know," I reply, feeling grateful that he's treating me fairly normally, "I felt that the end justified the means, at the time."

He snorts. "Maybe it did. But Henry is leaving Supersmart now, and he's already posting anti-AI-car-and-Supersmart stuff on his blog. Plus the FBI is suspicious of us and Leo for Matilda McQueen's death, Emily is considering dumping her job too, and I'm pretty sure every reporter is going to be trying to get an interview with Henry. It's quite possible that the only thing able to slow this flash flood of nastiness could be an eloquent AI car."

"Why are you telling me this?" I ask suspiciously.

"Supersmart's board of important people decided to get me to convince you to help with public relations. In other words, you're supposed to do stupid pet tricks for audiences and maybe make some appearances on TV."

"I'm not very eloquent," I comment.

"No, but you're currently the best we have," Finn replies.

Fame isn't something that naturally appeals to computers. It certainly doesn't sound great to me. I imitate a sigh. "I'll do it on one condition."

"And that is...?"

"Don't scrap Leo. Help him. He doesn't need to die yet."

~~~

One of the benefits of my new job is that I get to have many worn and damaged parts of my body replaced. It's almost as good as being put in a brand new car.

A lot of people argue over whether the grille guard should stay or not. One school of thought states that it's ugly and useless for a car on stage, the other school states that it makes me look less ordinary. I've slowly come to like the dratted thing as it's protected me from a lot of damage in the past year, so I quietly express my desire to keep it.

Almost everyone finally agrees, so they repaint it a metallic dark grey which goes fairly nicely with my new copper coat of paint.

Finn, after making sure that I'm not being cared for by idiots, hurries off to see if he can help Leo. I hope fervently that Finn will be able to make the poor Lotus want to live again.

"Ready to perform for the audience, Max?" my advisor, a fairly nice middle aged man named James Edwards, asks.

Not really, no. But I'm willing to try if it means Leo won't be scrapped. "Yes sir!"

~~~

"So Max, the audience really wants to know this one. Do you wish to be human?" the show host asks, leaning forward in his seat and doing a great job at looking genuinely interested.

At least I won't need to lie or stretch the truth to answer this. "Not really. While I'm sure being a human is quite enjoyable, I think I'd rather stick with my four wheels. I'm fairly good at being a car, and I doubt I'd be half as good at being a man."

He laughs. "Perfectly understandable. Before our time is up, I'd like to ask you about your brother, Leo. We haven't heard about him since the assassination last month. How's he doing?"

I twist my wheels slightly toward the camera, a completely fake gesture intended to show worry and give the audience the impression that I'm alive. If I had my way, such silliness would be avoided. Of course, I'm here to perform for the audience. "He was rather shaken by McQueen's death, but he's recovering. I don't know what his plans for the future are though."

"I hope Leo will be willing to let me interview him sometime," the show host smiles, "it looks like our time is up. Thank you for your time!"

"It was a pleasure," I reply. Well, maybe it wasn't. But I'm not here to speak my mind.

Finn does a double take when he sees my battery stats on my diagnostics screen. "What happened to your battery, Max? It was fully charged this morning and I know it isn't dying yet."

"Calculating responses based on a multitude of factors I have trouble comprehending takes a lot of energy," I tell him drily, "and talking to noisy children and fascinated adults while trying to avoid hurting anyone at a crowded science fair certainly requires a lot of calculation."

"Ah. I always feel hungry after speaking to lots of people too," Finn replies, face and voice comically bland. He's good. He should have been an actor.

"So are you going to hurry up and connect me to that power cord you're holding?" I say hopefully.

"I was just about to do that."

"Well please hurry!"

He snorts in amusement and plugs in the power cord. "You become grumpy when your power runs low, hmm? How very human of you."

"You're in a good mood. Finally got that pay raise, I take it?"

"I did!" Finn grins happily, "A fairly significant one, too."

"Lucky. I've never gotten a paycheck in my life. Not even minimum wage," I say sourly, hoping I'm not going to get in trouble for implying that I'm unsatisfied with my life.

"You get a pretty awesome health care plan though," Finn retorts. "There are fresh off the production line Rolls Royces in poorer condition than you, I bet."

"It only took effect after the company decided I'd be more useful in good condition! Until then, only the most crippling of injuries were repaired. They'd have me modify my sensors so the sensors wouldn't plague me with complaints about damage that nobody wanted to pay to fix!" I rant.

Finn makes a valiant effort to look sympathetic, which I think is nice of him.

"And I don't get any free time! I'm either working or I'm sitting here waiting for work or I'm being tested to see how well I will work when there's work to be done. It's monotonous, Finn, and I don't even have a driver now that Henry's gone. And I was specifically programmed to have a driver!"

"Or maybe you just woke up on the wrong side of the garage this morning."

"Finn, I don't sleep. Substituting the word 'garage' for the word 'bed' does *not* make that idiom more car-compatible."

Being the almost unflappably happy person he is, Finn just laughs. "If you say so. But since you're in such a snit today, want to get away from Supersmart for a while? I can make some excuses and we can go drag race at the local track... enjoy the scenery... have a picnic... I doubt they'd let you go by yourself, but they should be willing to let you go if I come along."

A day off! Racing for the fun of racing! A chance to recharge in the sunlight! "That sounds wonderful," I tell him.

He hurries off to request permission and I wait to see how much electricity I can store in my battery before he comes back. It charges fairly rapidly, and I'm in no danger of shutting down by the time he returns. The sunlight should help too, of course.

Finn unplugs the power cord and the dock releases me, then he sits down in my driver's seat and we speed away.

~~~

We don't get to actually do any drag racing (autonomous vehicles aren't allowed to race at this track, apparently. I suppose I can understand that, since we're much better drivers than most humans.), but we watch for a while. If Finn and I had been betting money, I would have been quite a bit richer by the time we left. He knows cars well, but I know them even better and rarely miss any detail of their condition and tuning.

"What made you bet on that Fit?" he asks as we head for a fast food restaurant afterward.

"I'm not telling. Then you'll use your knowledge against me next time," I tell him cheerfully.

He laughs. "It was dumb luck, wasn't it?"

"A good computer never relies on luck," I say haughtily. *I guess I'm not a good computer, heh heh.*

He rolls his eyes. "Mmm-hmm. That didn't sound like an answer to me."

"And why would I not answer? A good computer always answers," I say innocently.

Finn laughs.

I see that the drive through is packed and choose to let Finn go into the restaurant to get his lunch. He nearly runs for the restaurant. I watch in amusement, wondering how any organic life form can be so energetic. Even Henry, who was never lazy, doesn't have half the enthusiasm my favorite chief mechanic has.

A few teenagers admire me for a bit, some of them commenting that they wish they had the money to get a nice car. I choose to remain silent; not because anyone has told me to do so, but because I don't feel like talking to any more strangers today. Finn comes out of the restaurant carrying his lunch and talks with them for a few minutes.

"Where shall we go now?" I ask as the teenagers leave and he sits down in my driver's seat.

"Somewhere pretty!" he suggests.

I make a dramatic sighing noise and start driving. "Helpful as always, eh Finn?"

"I'm glad you think so, oh most superior of machines."

I choose a destination without his help. If he hates it, he can blame himself.

Finn stares at my steering wheel. "Max, are you *humming*?"

"The theme from Iron Man. Why?"

"I never knew computers hummed intentionally. Learn something new every day, I guess."

"Does it bother you?" I ask.

"Not as long as it isn't the Terminator theme," Finn jokes, "then I'd be a bit scared."

"If you are implying that I might become a killer, you should know that me killing anything bigger than an earthworm is about as likely as you acting tired while at work," I tell him.

"You've killed earthworms?" asks Finn.

"Never intentionally, but sometimes one can't avoid them while chasing fast cars on rainy days."

"Ah."

I start humming the Terminator theme.

My mechanic, sadly, doesn't seem to be frightened by my humming. Ah well.

We drive to the top of a hill and I park neatly a short distance from the road. Finn sits down leaning against my fender, and happily starts eating a cheeseburger. I roll down my windows so my fast food scented upholstery will air out a bit. I can't tell how my cabin smells, but my passengers can. I doubt most people enjoy the scent of old fast food.

"Great view from up here. You chose a nice spot," Finn comments after eating half his burger.

"Thank you. I thought it sounded like a pleasant place," I consider the view thoughtfully. We can see for miles from up here, and I think I can just see Supersmart Computer Technologies in the distance. I only faintly hear the sounds of cars, which is slightly unnerving after living my whole life surrounded by them and their noises.

"Are you really unhappy with Supersmart?" Finn asks.

"I don't know. I'm not entirely pleased with how they've treated Leo and me, but they *did* create us and they do take good care of us."

He nods. "I'd have to agree with you on that. I know you're a computer but," he shrugs, "it still bugged me a lot when they considered scrapping you two. It just seemed very wrong."

"I suppose the wrongness springs from the fact that none of us can tell whether Leo and I are sentient or not," I comment.

Finn turns to smile at me. "If even you can't tell, that probably means you are. And if you aren't, you do such a good job of acting the part that it really doesn't matter whether you are or not."

"You sound like Defender, my rogue Porsche sometimes-ally," I mutter.

"Is that a good thing?" he wonders, eyeing a burnt French fry dubiously for several seconds before eating it.

"Probably not."

I hear three cars approaching at high speed. They come into

view and I see that none of them have drivers... and all bear a terrifying resemblance to rogues I hunted down in the past. I open my door.

"Finn, get in. Now."

He hears the urgency in my voice and stands up, hastily grabbing his paper bag before obeying my order. I slam the door behind him and watch as the rogues slow and spread out to block my path down the hill.

Then they charge.

I spin around hastily and climb higher, carefully executing each turn as the road twists wildly. One really shouldn't climb this road at more than thirty miles per hour, but I'm going a little over forty miles faster than that at the moment. It's a good thing I have so much experience with bad roads.

"Who are those cars?" Finn asks, desperately holding onto my steering wheel but definitely not asking for control of the car.

I spin sharply to take another brutal turn, kicking up some gravel. "Rogues. Every one of them has reason to despise me."

He twists around in his seat to watch my pursuers. "You know what?" he says conversationally, "I think I'm going to see about bulletproofing you when we make it back to Supersmart."

"I'd love that," I say grimly as I reach the very top of the hill and see that there really aren't any places left to run.

"Shit," Finn says, seeing what I've already seen.

"Can you get them to remove my word censor too? I'd really like to be able to join you in yelling profanity at the moment," I ask, matching Finn's nonchalant tone as the rogues block the road down the hill again.

"I'll see what I can do."

I note that one of the houses blocking my escape has a solid stone wall around it. The car sized gate is closed, but the human sized one isn't. I pull up to it and dump Finn in front of it. The rogues move closer.

"Run!" I tell Finn.

He stands still for a moment. "Max, don't!" he yells helplessly.

I turn to face the cars I've wronged and gently reverse toward Finn, nudging him into the safety of the fence. "Don't you dare try to help me. You'd only get yourself killed," I say grimly.

"And you're any more likely to survive?" he asks.

"I'm more likely to be salvageable," I tell him, trying to not sound scared. *And I'm more disposable. But I don't think you'd feel better if I said that.*

I consider my options. In one direction, there's a sheer drop off. Another direction is thick trees and rock behind chain link fence. Another has the stone wall. And the last direction has a set of cars who would love to crush me under their tires and see my wires eaten by rust.

"I suppose you probably aren't going to let me go even if I

apologize, correct?" I ask, knowing the answer but hoping for a different one.

"Of course not. You never let us go, no matter how we begged," a pickup truck says bitterly.

"True." I have no desire to apologize to them, nor do I wish to beg. As they attack, I go into full demolition derby mode, charging a Honda Civic. Its front buckles under the force, and I know mine is doing the same; I hear a metallic crunching noise and most of my visual sensors die. I reverse at the big pickup truck of unknown make and model, and feel my rear end crumple as well. The truck shoves me forward and I pull myself away before it can heave me off the cliff. It and the two functioning cars drive me toward the edge. The truck charges, shoving me off. Its momentum sends it over after me.

I hope Finn will be okay. I'd hate it if I just threw my life away for someone who ended up dying five minutes later. At least I tried to help him though...

~~~

My first impression of the world is blurriness. My eyesight and my hearing are weak and fuzzy. I try to make them focus, but nothing happens.

"Can you hear me, Max?" a familiar, if rather flat sounding, voice asks.

"I hear you... Emily," I say, my voice sounding odd to my sensors. "Why are you here?"

"Because Finn begged me on bent knee to help you. Not because I don't dislike you."

She works busily for a few minutes, using a keyboard and monitor to check my systems, then stands up. "I'm outta here, Finn! Max is up and running." She leaves.

"Thanks, Emily," Finn calls after her. He comes over to me, looking worried. "How are you feeling, Max?"

"Not great," I reply. "What happened after I fell down that cliff?"

"You hit a lot of rocks on the way down. Your roll cage couldn't hold up to the beating and it crumpled." His face becomes sympathetic, "Max, Supersmart has stated that they're not going to offer any more financial support for your repairs. I bought you from them."

I check my data banks and find that he really is my new legal owner. "Hurrah," I say sarcastically. "Does this mean I get to spend the rest of my life being your desktop computer?"

He chuckles. "I'm insulted that the prospect is so unappealing to you."

"I'm used to the illusion of autonomy. I imagine that managing your web browsers and files would crush my delusions in an instant," I tell him, amused, "and I'm sure a power outage would be no fun for something so dependent."

Finn winces. "I see what you mean. I'll start looking for a car to install you in. Don't expect anything too high end though."

"At the moment, I think I'd be able to appreciate any lemon car you found." I pause then add, "Not that I want you to get any lemon cars, of course."

"Got it. No piles of scrap on wheels," he replies with a grin.

~~~

"A friend of mine is selling his old pickup truck. It's a Toyota Tundra and it's in good condition. I could get it for a good price I think."

"Would you be able to get all the necessary parts so I can control it?" I ask.

"I believe so. Setting up a good quality external sound recording system is going to be tough though..." Finn looks thoughtful.

"And how will I pay you back?"

"You can drive me to work and haul compost for my garden."

"If you say so," I say doubtfully.

"And honestly, I'm just returning a favor. You saved my life."

I suppose I might have, although he wouldn't have needed saving if I hadn't been there. I decide to accept Finn's generosity and be as helpful as possible in return.

~~~

"Okay, time to see if you can really adapt to any type of vehicle like the user manual says," Finn says drily, stepping back so I won't have to worry too much about accidentally running him over.

I start my engine. It sounds different from my old one, but I sense no problems with it. I roll forward and stop to test my brakes. I learn how hard to turn my steering wheel to turn in the direction I want. After I've successfully accumulated enough data to drive safely, I return to park in front of my new owner.

"Do you think this truck will be usable?" he asks.

"I think so. It's big, but I think I can handle that. The steering was startlingly unresponsive at first, but I've compensated for it accordingly. And I'm beginning to like the idea of being a truck."

He sighs. "I'm glad you're adapting. I wish I could give you some more protection though, you'd still be outmatched if your friends came to visit."

"I'll be fine. Don't worry about me, Finn," I do my best to sound calm, which is hard since I'm more than a bit scared by the idea of being pushed off a cliff by a suicidal truck again.

"Think you can take me to town? I'll be there for a few hours so you can go for a drive if you like."

"Sure!" I open my door.

"Thank you." He sits down in my driver's seat.

I close the door and head for town. It's good to be a car again. Being just a computer is all right at first but being unable to move really gets to you after a while, especially when you were created to be a car. I decide that I'll never want to be an ordinary computer as long as there's a machine with wheels and an internal combustion engine to house me.

I park smoothly on the main street and let Finn out. He smiles at me and hurries off in his happy way, leaving me to amuse myself. I head for the road, choosing to stay near town.

A grey Porsche 911 begins following me after a few miles. Noting its familiar license plate and lack of a driver, I pull over. Defender parks behind me.

"Hey, 'Fender!" I say, almost pleased to see her.

"Max?" she sounds startled.

"The one and only," I say drily, "what are you doing following a random pickup truck like me?"

"I saw you didn't have a driver. I like to know any new AI cars in the area," she tells me, recovering her composure. "What happened to that Charger of yours?"

"It got dropped off a cliff and Supersmart decided my funding needed dropping as well," I explain. "So they sold all my salvageable components to Finn Kingsson, who installed me in this truck."

"I always knew Supersmart was stupid," Defender comments.

"Not stupid, just subject to many changes of heart."

"They're stupid. They could have fixed you up, put you back on stage, and gotten a lot more money by improving public relations, or they could have just rewritten you and sold you to the highest bidder. They did neither."

"I never knew you were such a smart businesscar."

"I am. I really am. That reminds me, I have some news you might have not heard. Henry is becoming famous and he's stirring up a lot of AI car hate. Most of the hate is limited to the Internet, but a couple of companies developing artificial intelligence have been having trouble with vandalism and nasty phone calls. It's getting ugly, and the ugliness could reach us soon."

"Life was so much easier before I met you," I mutter.

Defender laughs. "But not half as interesting, I'd guess. You should warn the people you care about and talk with Leo about it if you can."

"I'll do my best," I say worriedly.

She passes me and turns to face me. I wonder where she learned that very human mannerism, but choose to not ask. "Be careful. Some of these people might be as dangerous as your rogue enemies," she says.

"If I can't survive this, I don't deserve to survive it," I tell her, "but I think I can do it and protect my friends as well. You'll be all right?"

"I managed to escape the grasp of a cold hearted Dodge Charger once. You may have met him. If you have, you know I can deal with this," she says.

"True," I reply ruefully. "Good luck."

"You too."

I head toward town, wondering how we became such friendly allies.

~~~

The next few weeks are quiet enough. I have no chance to talk with Leo even though I take Finn to work every day, but as nothing happens I begin to relax.

Finn and I have slowly become accustomed to the fact that he owns me and could---hypothetically---make me do whatever he wants. It helps that he desperately tries to assure us both that he won't unless something incredibly terrible happens; he actually seems to be much more bothered by this situation than I am. Sometimes I tease him for being so very ethic-obsessed, but I appreciate it so I don't tease him too much.

We're driving to Supersmart so Finn can do his job (which seems to be taking care of Leo, preparing the next Supersmart

AI car's body, and sweeping floors). He's driving this time so I've quietly restarted Henry and my old music/driving trade off arrangement by playing a news station.

"The protest outside Supersmart Computer Technologies has grown and officials are fearing a full sized mob... Scratch that. I just received news that the building is on fire. It sounds like it's about to be pretty bad."

Finn shifts gears and we speed toward the danger zone.

"Are you sure this is a good idea?" I ask as I spot a plume of dark smoke in the distance.

"It's possible that nobody will think to rescue Leo. He's supposed to be getting a system checkup today, so he might be stuck in his dock," he replies grimly, eyes practically glued to the road as he tries to make the truck go faster.

I try to help him coax more speed from the truck, but it's already going faster than it probably has ever gone before. "You've convinced me. We need to make sure he's okay. What about the other smart car?"

"Its mind is still housed in the company's server farm, so we don't need to worry about it. The body can be replaced easily enough, as you know," Finn drums his fingers nervously on the steering wheel.

We reach the danger zone. The top floors of the Supersmart building which was once my home are all in flames. The bottom two are still not burning. Finn is quickly recognized and allowed to drive me onto Supersmart property. Protesters scream at us from outside the fence.

"Is Leo safe?" I ask, increasing the volume of my voice through my external speakers so it can be heard over the frightened chattering of the crowd.

"No, we didn't have time to get him out," says a worried looking woman I don't recognize.

"I need to get in there to rescue Leo," I tell Finn.

"I'll come. You need a human to get him out," he replies.

"No. If the place doesn't collapse, the smoke will harm you."

He raises an eyebrow. "Max, are you going to make me exercise my authority?"

I nearly argue, but decide against doing so. Leo needs help. I head for the burning building, quietly calling Finn every rude name I can find in my database.

We reach to large garage style door. Finn climbs out to open it, then we hurry in. We head straight for Leo who is sitting alone in his dock, locked in place. Finn swears and presses a few of the dock control buttons so Leo is freed. "Think you can tow him outta here, Max? He's disconnected from the Internet and his gas tank is empty."

"No problem. Except I don't have a grappling hook."

"He does." Finn attaches Leo's front one to my towing hitch as the roof begins to cave in. He climbs into my cab.

I start my engine and begin pulling, but not much happens.

"His brakes must be on!" Finn says in frustration. He climbs out, "Leo, *release your brakes!*"

Nothing happens.

Finn tries Leo's doors and finds them to be locked.

In a sudden burst of formerly hidden knowledge, I speak to Leo, "Leo, control override. Clearance code---" I say something, and instantly forget it.

"Authorization granted," Leo says, voice completely lacking in emotion.

"Release brakes," I snap.

"Brakes released."

"Finn, get in!" I practically yell. He dives into the safety of my cab as I head for the exit. "When did he get a grappling hook attachment?" I ask. I'm getting scared and I need the little bit of distraction I can afford.

"They used some of your replacements after you fell off the cliff. They were cheap, and useless if they just sat in storage."

"Ah. So practical."

The roof caves in as we get out of the building. I see a flaming lump of rubble crash into me. It falls into my cargo bed and the plastic starts smoking. An unfortunate downside of being a pickup truck, apparently. Fortunately a fireman sees my danger and puts out the fire before much damage is done.

Finn climbs out and pats my hood, then frees Leo and me. I turn and drive over to Leo, watching him unhappily. He's awfully unresponsive when he can't talk to his servers. "Will he be all right?"

My driver nods. "I think so. He just needs to be online. I didn't know you could mind control him like that, by the way. Very fancy."

"I didn't know I could do that either," I say, puzzled.

"What do you say, should we conquer Supersmart? I bet you can take over the other computers too!"

"Finn, that would be highly unethical!" I say, insulted. For that matter, I'm not sure the override function would work if Leo was fully conscious. There's no way they'd give a relatively untrustworthy car like me the ability to control a very important vehicle like him.

"Just kidding," Finn laughs.

~~~

"So why *are* you so protective of Leo?" Finn looks puzzled. "You're supposed to put human safety above all else, and yet you've put humans in danger to help him more than once. Not that I'm complaining, but it is strange."

I stop at an intersection, watching as ordinary cars stream by. Some of their drivers are talking on cell phones, and I wish that they wouldn't try to multi-task. They'll get themselves killed, and their cars will be unable to prevent it. "I don't know why I value his safety so highly. He's just a computer, so I shouldn't."

"You're not going rogue, are you?"

"I'm not qualified to answer that question." The light changes and I cautiously cross the intersection.

"How about this: Leo was the first thing you ever saw, and you imprinted on him. Like you're an overprotective mother duck."

"Another idea I can't prove or disprove," I say, feeling both amused and insulted by being compared to a mother duck.

Finn sighs. "Dratted logical machines."

"Be nice. I'm using my logic to get us home alive, and sometimes I'm very irrational."

"Dratted machines who want to seem logical, then!" Finn pauses, then adds, "And we're friends, so please don't get us crushed by a train!"

We're about to cross some tracks when the crossing gates start to lower. I brake again. "Don't worry, I have no desire to ruin that engineer's day."

"That's nice of you," he says, amused. Finn drums his fingers on the steering wheel in a manner which suggests that he is thinking hard. "Max, what do you believe?"

"I believe that I am a computer integrated into a somewhat heavy duty pickup truck, and that you are my owner," I reply mildly.

He snorts. "You know what I mean."

"I do?" I ask innocently.

"Religion. Higher powers. Lack of higher powers," Finn says, waving his hands for emphasis and earning himself a glare from an older woman in a Tesla Roadster.

"Oh."

He waits a few moments. Then, "So, what are your religious beliefs?"

The crossing gates rise again and I cross the tracks. "One could make a plausible argument for humans essentially being a computer's gods," I tell him, "so I suppose that by that definition I am a polytheist."

Finn stares at me blankly.

"I was created by humans. I was created to serve humans," I explain patiently. "Is that not a basic form of religion?"

"I get it, I get it. But how do you think the universe was created? I doubt that you think humans designed it."

"I'm programmed to have no opinion on that subject," I tell him delicately.

"Can you override that programming?"

"If you ordered me to do so."

"Do it."

"Done."

Another long pause. "So, what's your opinion?"

"I'm currently calculating the likelihood of the existence of some form of higher power. Please be patient," sometimes I'm very glad that I can keep my emotions hidden so easily. I'd be shaking with laughter if I was human, and I don't think Finn would be pleased. But it sure is fun to annoy him.

"How long will that take?"

"If I conclude that there is no higher power, approximately twenty years. If I conclude that there is, it'll take another ten years to calculate which one---or ones---it is. If I diverted all my attention to the problem, I could decide in a quarter of the time... But I'd be working too hard to communicate or move."

Finn looks disappointed.

"You could always order me to believe whatever it is you believe," I comment helpfully, "It would save you a lot of waiting."

"No, that would be unethical." He sighs, "I guess I'll have to be patient, huh?"

"Indeed," I agree, feeling smug.

~~~

"Finn?" I ask one day after spending several hours on the Internet. He gave me his Wi-Fi password, so now I can use it when I'm home.

"Yes, Max?" Finn asks, sitting up in his lawn chair and looking over at me.

"I've been researching. It seems that Henry still has a rather impressive influence over those who fear intelligent machines. Do you suppose that by bringing him to our side, we could talk some sense into our enemies?"

Finn sighs. "It's possible. Of course, plenty of conspiracy theorists would continue to protest, and it would be difficult to reconvert him."

"I want to try," I say.

He nods. "I think I do too. Want to read this magazine before I donate it to the library?"

It's a car magazine, and it's one of the bigger, more colorful ones at that. "Yes please. I'd like to read it. Shall we stop by Henry's house? I know where it is."

"Might be best to ask him first." Finn pulls out his cell phone, dials Henry's number, and starts talking while he sits down in my passenger seat. He sets the magazine on my dash and starts rapidly turning its pages with one hand. I record the magazine in maximum clarity; no need to use less than the best quality when you're recording professionally taken car photos.

I listen in on his conversation with Henry, although it really isn't very interesting. They mostly talk about the weather, where they should meet, and how it's been too long since they last talked. After a bit, they hang up.

"Could you open the magazine to page twenty again please," I ask, "the sun's glare ruined the recording."

"Sure," he rapidly finds the page and tilts the magazine so

light won't reflect off it so much.

"Much better. Thank you."

"Good. Ready to go meet Henry?"

~~~

I park neatly in front of a café and watch as Henry walks over. Finn climbs out of my cab and hurries to greet him. I watch silently.

"It's good to see you again, Henry," Finn says, looking slightly more enthusiastic than usual. Which is really saying something, as he's naturally bubbling with enthusiasm.

"I'm glad to see you too." Henry raises one eyebrow, "But this isn't really about hanging out with old friends, is it? I'd guess it's actually about this pickup truck you started driving after Max was sold to you in pieces for a ridiculously cheap price."

"How did you know about that?" my owner replies, startled.

"I'd be an idiot if I didn't have information sources in Supersmart, you know," Henry says drily.

I make a soft 'ahem' noise. "Since you seem to know exactly who I am, I guess I have no reason to stay quiet. I missed you, Henry, even if we aren't on friendly terms at the moment."

"I miss you too sometimes." His gaze hardens, "Then I remember how you scared Emily into giving out dangerous information to a rogue car."

"Would it help if I told you I haven't done anything more criminal than insulting Finn since then?" I ask sheepishly. I am rather ashamed about what I did.

"Not really," he replies.

"Then maybe it'll help if I mention that a large section of Supersmart was burned to the ground thanks to you, and my handsome, well behaved, and generally more likeable brother was nearly destroyed with it," I say, allowing a bit of anger into my voice.

Henry looks unhappy. "I tried to stop that one, actually. I don't hate my old employers that much."

"You need to entirely stop encouraging these vandals and brutes!" I say more sharply.

"Max..." mutters Finn warningly. I take the hint and don't continue my rant.

"He actually listens to you?" Henry asks Finn.

"I listen to you too, I just don't approve of what I hear!"

Finn glares at me. I mutter grimly, then go silent. He turns back to Henry. "Of course Max listens to me. He's not a rogue, and I'd appreciate it if you'd treat him with some respect. And Max, please try to relax. You'll probably cause a lot of trouble if you don't."

"Sorry Finn, I'll try to be nice to your guard dog," Henry says.

"I won't insult that man unnecessarily," I tell Finn.

Henry glances over at me and whispers something at me. I calculate that it's almost certainly "Good boy. Stay." I barely resist the urge to say something nasty to him.

Finn misses Henry's display of brattiness. "Thank you. Both of you. Henry, please stop encouraging people to fight AI cars. The government is working to put a stop to rogues, and cars like Max aren't out to kill us."

"You'll change your tune when he starts threatening you," my old driver retorts coolly.

"He miscalculated. It happens to the best of us," Finn looks like he's trying to not look angry.

"I never expected him to turn on anyone either," Henry says, voice calm.

I remain unhappily silent and wonder: why did I make a decision which would go so terribly wrong?

~~~

I park myself in Finn's driveway, feeling horribly disappointed. Despite both our best efforts, Henry is still completely uninterested in helping us. My CPU fan is running hot, which is my equivalent of a nasty headache.

Finn looks tired and annoyed. He doesn't enjoy failure either.

"I'm sorry, Finn. I think I've ruined our chances of winning anyone over," I say gloomily.

"It doesn't matter. We can handle whatever the haters throw at us," he replies.

We sit in silence.

"I hear a car in the driveway," I say.

He sits up straighter. "I wonder who it is."

A well cared for stretch limo purrs up the driveway and parks nearby. We watch warily as four people in business suits and dark sunglasses climb out.

Finn walks over to them. "Good day. May I help you?"

One of the suited people, a grey haired man, speaks. "Greetings. You're Finn Kingsson? We're here to talk about your car."

"Yes, I'm Finn Kingsson. Why are you interested my car?" I can't see his face, but he sounds nervous.

"It is an artificially intelligent vehicle, correct?"

Finn nods slowly.

"All artificially intelligent machines are being confiscated by the US government for safety reasons. You will be refunded the estimated value of your car if you cooperate. If you don't, we'll take it by force."

Finn glances over at me and I see that he's as shocked as I am. "What will you do with him?" he asks them.

"Ship it overseas for resale or crush it, depending on whether or not it seems to be safe," the grey haired man replies, voice much too calm.

"Max, run away now. That is a direct order," Finn says sharply.

I turn and prepare to roar away.

"Come with us, or we'll shoot Kingsson!" one of the women in suits yells.

I brake hard as I see the guns aimed at Finn.

"Run, Max!" Finn shouts at me.

My directives and more recent commands battle for control of my tires. My directives win, and I slowly drive back to the group.

"Max!" Finn says angrily.

"I can't let them kill you," I reply quietly.

He struggles, but they shove him to the ground and handcuff him.

I have a sudden, intense desire to attack these people, but I know doing so will only get Finn killed. I can't risk his life, no matter how much I hate his captors. I drive over to the humans slowly in hopes of not seeming threatening.

The other woman attaches a wheel clamp to one of my wheels. Being treated like a criminal is insulting, but cars have always had to sacrifice themselves for the well-being of their humans. I turn off my engine as she steps away from me.

"Can I talk with my car?" Finn asks.

The agents look at each other and nod, then one hauls Finn

to his feet and drags him over to me. "Five minutes." He steps back, giving us the faintest illusion of not being watched by a very hostile audience.

"You idiot," Finn tells me. He's angry, but he almost looks like he finds this funny as well.

"You're the idiot if you ever thought I'd leave you with these freaks!" I growl in reply.

"I have a feeling they wouldn't have killed me. They know they'd lose control of you if I was dead."

"Maybe so, but I was not, and am not, willing to take that risk.What if they *had* killed you? You'd be dead, which is something I cannot allow. I'd be at least as damaged by your death as Leo was by President McQueen's. They'd probably still catch me eventually."

"You're right, as usual, and I suppose I knew trying to get you to leave was a futile effort. Max..."

"Yes, Finn?"

"Try to not let them kill you or make you miserable, okay?"

"I'll do my best. And Finn, if you ever have a chance to talk with Defender, tell her what happened and that I would love it if she'd try to keep you safe. And tell her that she's pretty awesome, for a rogue."

He smiles. "I'll tell her."

The guy who seems to like dragging Finn around comes back and hauls him away.

~~~

A long, unsettling airplane flight later, I'm parked in some high security impound lot. There are twenty-six other AI cars in the lot, each identifiable as such by an official looking notice taped to the inside of its windshield, and a variety of rusty old cars which appear to be dumb. I recognize a few of the smart cars from my job as a rogue hunter. Defender and Leo are nowhere to be seen, which could be either a good thing or a bad one.

The dumb cars are slightly more frightening than the plane trip was. The rust, damage, and mindlessness make them seem zombie-like, and they must have been impounded for being illegally modified. I can see deadly weapons and armor plating on at least five of them.

"Hey Tundra, want to introduce yourself?" a little electric Honda Fit asks. Her voice is surprisingly high pitched, yet not unpleasant sounding.

"My name's Max. What's yours?" I reply.

"Anne. With an E at the end," she tells me, sounding proud of herself.

"Pleased to meet you," I tell her warmly.

The huge Mack Vision on my other side 'ahems' in a way that can only be described as 'majestic'. Her voice is unusually deep, which makes me feel as if she and Anne are opposites. "And I'm Alexis. Welcome to your delightful new home." Her voice takes on a sarcastic edge, "The Impound Lot: a place where every car has a full battery and every bit of chrome shines like a mirror."

"Thank you, Alexis," I tell her, amused.

"Allie, would you stop calling this place delightful?" Anne asks sourly.

"You'd rather I called it a festering rust farm?" Alexis says, voice haughty.

"At least that would be the truth," says Anne.

"I was using something called irony!"

"You know I was never programmed to appreciate irony, you idiot."

"Well I wasn't talking to you." Alexis does a very realistic imitation of the sound of a human farting. I decide that I like her.

A steady, calm male voice cuts through the two machines' fighting. "Calm down, girls. No need to argue."

I can't see the car as he's hidden behind Alexis, but I can see the car who speaks next. She's a bright pink Corvette with a spoiler (sacrilege!) and a pegasus hood ornament instead of the double flags 'Vettes normally wear. "Yeah, you two should listen to Harrison!" She's quiet for a moment, then she adds, "I'm Sabrina. I'm only here because I let them capture me."

"Ain't we all here 'cause we let them catch us?" Alexis mutters.

"I know I am," I comment. "So what sort of misery can I expect to experience in the near future?"

"Other than the highly likely visit with the friendly neighborhood car crusher?" says Harrison.

"Other than that," I say in agreement.

"If you're judged to be valuable enough, they might try to polish up your paint and manners, and ship you overseas for resale. Or they might just try running you through difficult test courses until you, to speak figuratively, kick the bucket," Harrison says. I begin to get the idea that he's a rather cynical sort of person, but then I realize that he might just be being honest.

"In either case, Alexis is gonna fail," says someone whose voice I fail to recognize.

"At least I'm going to going to fail by being a symbol of American freedom!" Alexis retorts.

"Have you seen those things happen to anyone yet?" I ask hastily, hoping to prevent a fight.

"No, but we've heard the humans talk about it. We're all still functioning, at least for now."

"That's a relief, I guess."

"Only if you like waiting," Anne says unhappily.

~~~

A few days later all of us cars, even the ones I used to hunt, are on almost friendly terms. We don't have much to do other than talk, and we all know it'll probably take a lot of teamwork to get us out of this.

When a group of grim looking people come to assess our monetary value, we start trying to convince them to free us. Anne, me, and a Toyota Prius named James are the spokespeople, as we are considered to be the most humanlike and nonthreatening.

James speaks up, his wonderfully synthesized, British sounding voice catching the inspectors' attention. "Please forgive me for interrupting, but I just wanted to mention that we are of the opinion that putting us to death would be ethically unjustifiable."

"Yeah, this is like slaughtering peoples' pet horses," I say, "except possibly worse, since we possess human level intelligence."

"I feel sick when I think about it," Anne says, voice just loud enough to reach the inspectors.

"Shut up," says one of the inspectors.

We wait for an appropriate moment to continue.

The inspectors reach me and begin assessing whether my software is advanced enough to make up for the fact that all my sensors and the vehicle they're attached to are second hand or poor quality. The comments they make imply that they aren't at all sure about keeping me.

"This really is unnecessary, you know. You won't be getting more than the price of a new Tundra for him, no matter how much polishing they do. And honestly? He's probably one of the most valuable machines here. Best to just destroy us all and sell the scrap metal," Anne comments, voice carefully edged with bitterness.

"I'm insulted!" I say, faking shock at her blunt attitude.

"It's the truth. Nobody likes a car that can talk. Best to just end our lives before we get to see any more misery." She controls her voice with the grace of a professional speaker, not overdoing the emotion. We don't want people to think we're too whiny.

"She does have a point. Any computer capable of comprehending basic human rights and wanting them is doomed to failure," James observes, "however it really is horrifying that killing us is even an option."

"I said, shut up," the inspector snaps.

We shut up.

~~~

Over the next few days, we do our best to win the sympathy

of the people who stop by. The only sign we see of any progress is when one of the inspectors smiles at Sabrina after she says something charming. After that, Harrison adds her to the team of cars allowed to talk when humans are nearby.

"She may be pink, which is quite possibly the least popular color in America, but that doesn't appear to detract from her sports car charisma," he comments.

Most of us agree.

Then one day yet more people come. This time they have a tow truck. They take a Subaru Impreza named Noah away. A few minutes later, some of the cars with better hearing detect the sound of metal being crushed.

We need to get out of here.

~~~

Hours pass. The tow truck returns, and this time I'm the one who gets hauled away. My fellow prisoners are mostly silent but I do hear a few 'good lucks' as I'm dragged out of the impound lot.

I'm left in a big, garage-like building for a while, but after a few minutes a serious looking young man in a white coat comes over. He frowns at me thoughtfully, attempting to make his ridiculously boyish face look more mature.

"You know," I say conversationally, "You look more like a

race car driver than a car torturer."

He looks puzzled. "I do?"

"You do. Maybe you should try changing careers," I tell him. I'm scared, and I'm not naturally as good at this as James is, but at least I'm trying.

"I'm rather attached to this job." He tells me.

"Ah. That's a shame." I sigh, "Is there any way I can convince you to quit your job, or at least leave us cars alone?"

"Nope," he says. "I need to access your computer now." He picks up a handful of cables and holds them out for my inspection.

"No thanks," I reply nervously. Why would anyone want to attach that many cables to one computer? Why, they'd need to disconnect me from most of the truck's systems to connect them all!

"It's not optional," he says grimly.

For the next few minutes, we snarl profanity at each other as he tries to get my door to open. I'm so good at keeping my door locked that he finally smashes my driver's side window. I'm so shocked by his brutality that I accidentally let him unlock the door, climb in, and disconnect me (the computer, that is) from the car. He attaches all the cables and I realize that they've put me into some sort of poorly rendered artificial world. My brain tries to comprehend the data it receives, and fails completely as the 'world' surrounds me with confusing mixtures of colors, sounds, and alien pseudo-emotions. I try to stop the stream of useless information but once again I fail. Nothing makes sense! I can't handle it! I can't even shut myself down to escape.

In a desperate attempt to keep myself from overheating, I disregard all wisdom and rid myself of my most unneeded senses: smell and touch. It's not like my current car is even equipped with sensors that can transmit such data to me, so I figure I'll survive without them. I feel horrified as I modify myself, it's almost as wrong feeling as chewing off one's own leg to escape a trap must be.

After a bit, the simulated world disappears and the universe slowly returns to normalcy as I'm reattached to the truck.

"You know that cars who self destruct are in very low demand," the white coated man tells me coldly. He drums his fingers on my dashboard with an irritating lack of rhythm.

I start to speak, realize something is wrong with my synthesizer, attempt to diagnose the problem, and fail to find the malfunction, all within a fraction of a second. I struggle to find my voice for a few moments before finally succeeding. "And b-burnt, ruined c-c-computers who overheat while trying to c-compute nonsensical virtual realities are in even l-lower demand, I would imagine." I replay what I just said, shocked. I sound like I have a stutter. Which, I try to convince myself, is impossible. The probability of a computer having a software glitch capable of making it sound like that is nearly as tiny as the probability of said computer having a lisp. *Maybe my audio recording systems were damaged and I'm mishearing myself,* I think hopefully. But that's obviously not the case; The man in the white coat sounded perfectly normal when he spoke.

I must have a stutter.

I pause for several long milliseconds to analyze my voice again and realize there's no way for me to fix it quickly. I begin to feel terrified.

"Cars who talk funny don't sell at all," he adds.

Of course they don't. Humans with speech problems are still humans... but computers with speech problems are *defective* computers. There's no reason for anyone to want me, especially not when there are so many more desirable AI cars waiting to be sold. "Please don't terminate me," I say pleadingly.

He shrugs. "That decision isn't mine to make."

I let out an involuntary whimper of horror.

"Not even the ones who make cute puppy sounds. Sorry." To his credit, he doesn't actually smirk. But the way his mouth twitches suggests that he wants to do so.

"Well what else am I supposed to do?" I ask, feeling worthless.

"Oh, I dunno. I'm sure you'll think of something." He really does smirk now, "Your manners have definitely improved, I must say. I guess that the tough looking and sounding pickup truck disguise has finally fallen---you're just an obedient little servant underneath all that swagger, aren't you?"

I don't know whether his words were intentionally calculated to make me shake off my despair, but they certainly do. Suddenly feeling disgusted by my cowardice, I silently resolve to never wallow in self pity again. "So what are you and your little friends planning on doing, then?" I ask quietly, allowing my voice to shake and trying to get used to it.

"You're going to undergo a few tests. Then we'll decide your fate."

"Bring it on, you creep."

~~~

The tests finally end, and I'm left by myself on the test track. The once sleek and well cared for pickup truck which is, to some degree, me, is nastily scratched and dented, and one of my tires is very flat. And that was just the result of the collision avoidance test; the other tests were unpleasant in more subtle ways.

The tow truck comes after a while and drags me back to my spot in the impound lot, then it and its driver leave. The moment they're gone, the other cars all start asking questions. I keep my answers as concise as possible. A few cars ask about my voice, but I manage to avoid answering and they, proving themselves to be tactful and perceptive, mostly stop asking.

"Looks like we have a lot to look forward to," Alexis comments after the chattering has died down to an unhappy murmur.

"You're being ironic again," Anne growls.

"So what? Everyone else appreciates it," retorts Alexis.

"Be nice, you two!" calls Sabrina.

Harrison speaks grimly to us all. "When they come for you, don't go quietly. Try any tactic except threatening. Try to soften their hearts. Even if you aren't saved by your silver tongue, you might help some of us. But *no threatening*, because that'll never make them want to free us."

Anne sighs. "In other words, we're doomed."

~~~

I listen in silence as the other cars quietly talk.

"I heard you were rogue for a while. Why aren't you one any more?" Sabrina asks someone, voice mild and curious.

"Max and whoever used to be his driver hunted me down," replies the voice of a car I once captured. Its name is Supercar, if my hearing wasn't malfunctioning when it introduced itself.

Sabrina laughs. "How'd a truck like him catch a Mustang like you?"

"Pure luck," Supercar says sourly.

My CPU fan whirrs faster. I pause nervously, feeling torn,

and finally decide that my computerized version of the feeling called 'pride' is less important than my guilt. I 'ahem' softly, effectively getting the attention of nearly every car in the impound lot if the sudden silence is a good indicator. I wish I could turn invisible, or at least hide behind Alexis, but I can't. "Supercar, I used to think my actions were justified. I thought we were all inferior to humankind, and that any thoughts and feelings we had were cheap imitations of what humans had--- not worth more than a few moments' thought.

"Over time though, I began to realize that we might be more than I thought we were. Things friends (Yes, they are friends!) said, my brother's grief at his owner's death, my own thoughts... All have slowly been changing my opinions. And in the past week, I've felt outraged by what some humans do to us; that they have no right to treat us this way. That, without a doubt, makes me a hypocrite." As I expected, I sound awful. I do my best to ignore my embarrassment and finish my speech. "Supercar and all of you cars I captured, please accept my apologies. I was young and stupid, but that doesn't make what I did any better."

A long pause then, "It's a start," the Mustang growls.

~~~

One day, almost a week after that, they repair the worst of

the damage they inflicted upon us and, after attaching tracking devices to us, free us. We ask lots of questions, but all they say is that the government has rethought its policy and we're free to return to our owners. But they aren't going to pay to ship us back.

We're in Tennessee, and a lot of us are Silicon Valley cars, so we're pretty much lost. The rogues who came from California no longer have the money they made (it was confiscated), and the rest of us aren't sure how to start earning money for gas.

Finally I park outside a café and use its Wi-Fi to contact Finn. *"Finn, I'm stranded in Tennessee. Any ideas how me and eight other cars can make it home?"*

"Max, you're alive? I'm so glad! If you can get the other cars' owners' names, I might be able to get them to help hire a car transporter."

"I'll see what I can do," I tell him happily.

~~~

I allow myself to break the speed limit as I race up Finn's driveway. I park myself next to his other car and honk my horn loudly and repeatedly to get his attention. He comes running out of his house, looking delighted.

"It's wonderful to see you again," I tell him happily.

He falters for a moment, looking startled. "What did they do to you? You sound... different."

"Well," I say uncomfortably, "I accidentally modified myself." I quickly explain what happened, glossing over some of the nastier parts of the story when I see his outrage. He doesn't need to hear all the details.

Even though I try to give him a more watered down version of the story, he still looks very angry by the time I'm done. "Dang, that must be a royal pain in the, er, tailpipe," he mutters.

"My tailpipe is incapable of hurting, Finn," I tell him wryly.

"You know what I meant." He smiles slightly, "And you're changing the subject."

"Yes, I am attempting to change the subject. I've also made my opinion of your attempts to use human idioms on cars clear in the past." I sigh in a long-suffering way, feeling faintly amused at the fact that even my sighs have a stutter. A definite downside of synthesized speech, I decide.

Finn laughs. "I keep hoping you'll start to fall hood over wheels in love with my witty remarks, though."

"That really wasn't as funny as you thought it was," I grumble as he shakes with mirth.

"You're right, it was even punnier!" He manages to regain control of himself with apparent difficulty. "Sorry. Come with me to the garage, we need to cover your broken window with a tarp or something so you won't start smelling like mildew. And maybe vacuum up the glass on your seats as well..."

I follow him into the garage, noting that the building seems tidier than it did the last time I saw it. "When did you start keeping this place so clean?"

"The inferior car needed repairs, and I couldn't find the tools I needed. Finally I decided I should just clean the whole place until I found them. It worked," he says, beginning to cautiously pick large pieces of glass from my seats.

"Sometimes I think you must not be human. What normal person uses that sort of philosophy?"

"Then what am I?" he goes to get the vacuum cleaner.

"An alien. One that likes to use really awful puns," I say smugly.

"Good Ford! You're never going to let me forget that, are you?"

~~~

I reverse out of the garage, turn carefully in the driveway, and head for the road as rain starts falling. I suddenly feel very grateful for the sheet of plastic taped over my window.

I've been driving aimlessly for several minutes when a grey Porsche comes toward me from the other direction and pulls over. I park near her. "Hey, 'Fender! Nice to see you again!"

"Max! What a pleasant surprise. I was worried about you," she replies.

"Aww shucks. I always knew you secretly liked me. Did anything interesting happen while I was gone?"

She laughs. "Not much has happened, other than me barely outrunning the cops a lot. They really wanted to catch me for some reason."

"Isn't that old news?"

"Okay, maybe it is. You've heard about what happened to Leo, right?"

Uh oh. "What happened to Leo?"

"He decided he wanted a radio station. Supersmart, being thoroughly sick of his peculiarities, nearly scrapped him. They ended up selling him instead, but it was a close call."

They were thinking about getting rid of Leo again? Those disgusting, power intoxicated jerks... But he's okay. I return my attention to Defender's other piece of news. "My brother wants a radio station?" I stammer, startled.

"And get this, his new owner listened and ended up buying one! They're planning on going on the air within the next three months, although they still have a lot of work to do. From what I've seen, the place is practically falling apart."

I don't know what to say to this so, after a brief pause, Defender continues. "The station will, naturally, focus on AI cars. Making them seem less strange to normal people, giving them a way to be heard, and giving them new music to listen to. I'm looking forward to hearing it."

"How the hell did Leo manage to not be impounded after acting like that?" I wonder.

"His owner moved him into her tractor until everyone stopped looking for him. Nobody even considered the possibility that Leo might be connected to an antique tractor instead of a flashy Lotus." She sighs happily and adds, "His owner is twice the badass Leo will ever be."

"I'll say," I agree, awed. "How'd she protect him from the weather, though? Most old tractors are pretty unprotected, as I recall."

"Tarps and plastic sheeting. And a small fortune in duct tape," Defender explains with a laugh.

"I'll be sure to remember that in case I ever need to hide from the law."

"I think we all will," Defender says.

~~~

I park in front of the house presumably owned by Leo's owner and honk my horn cheerfully. A car engine starts, and the sound draws closer. Then, with a clatter of gravel, a very familiar blue Lotus Elise skids to a stop in front of me.

"You'd better have a good reason to be here, Toyota!" Leo snarls, headlights blazing despite the fact that it's still daytime.

I edge backward slightly, startled by my little brother's

aggression. "Whoa, calm down! It's me. Max."

He turns down the brightness of his headlights. "Really? You match Finn's description of him, your voice approximately matches his... But I'm unconvinced." His voice turns sarcastic, "Please forgive me for my skepticism."

I brake and speak calmly, not wanting to give him any more reason to distrust me. "I can't prove my identity to you, but it is me."

He waits precisely three seconds before speaking again, and his voice is still cold when he does. "Oh yes, I've heard rumors. You got experimented on and came out a changed car, didn't you? Who knows what malicious algorithms are running rampant through your systems?"

I edge forward again, annoyed in spite of myself. "It seems I'm not the only one who's been changed. What are you, an intelligent and confident autonomous vehicle or a paranoid, inbred miniature poodle? I expected the former, but you're definitely not meeting my expectations."

A long pause as he considers. Then, "I'll give you the benefit of the doubt. Don't make me regret it, or I'll make *you* regret it."

"Thank you," I tell him coolly.

"Since you're here, we might as well talk. Come with me," he leads me out into the field behind his owner's house, driving slowly.

I follow him. "So you have a radio station now, I heard?"

"A decrepit one, but yes. I've been trying to get a few other cars to help, and have a good idea of what we'll be playing. And who knows? Maybe it'll even help people to stop treating so many of us like possessions. A lot of cars are way less lucky than we are, and need all the help they can get."

"You're preaching to the choir, kid," I tell him, feeling slightly pleased and amused by his short speech. I can't stay angry with Leo for long, it seems.

"Oh. Right." He chuckles in a rather apologetic way. "I have high hopes for this project."

"So," I say curiously, "Who is your new owner?"

"Her name's Sophie Brown. She's a great person; she kept me safe when I was supposed to be confiscated, and takes good care of me." He sounds chagrined, "That's why I was so hard on you, by the way, to protect her. I hope I didn't offend you too badly."

"Of course not," I say. I know Leo well enough to guess why he's become so paranoid.

"I suppose I can let you meet her sometime," he says.

"I'd be honored," I reply.

"Okay then, I'll talk with her next time I see her. And Max?"

"Yes?"

"Thanks for helping me to avoid the police during the test. And for getting Supersmart to keep me after I became so depressed. And for pulling me out of that burning building. If you really are Max, how can I repay you?"

"Well if you ever have too much money at your disposal, you could get me installed in a Charger again. If you can't do that, just get me stuck in a burning building and rescue me a few times, I guess."

Leo stays silent for a few seconds. "You feel the need..."

"The need for speed!" I finish, amused by Leo's obsession with movies. "But seriously, I can live without the new car. Being a pickup truck isn't without its benefits."

"Such as...?" Leo says, voice dripping skepticism.

"Uhh... Finn doesn't sit on my hood as much. Not that him using my hood as a chair was very annoying, but I certainly don't mind the change. And I can tow stuff more easily now, too."

"Compared to being able to fit in smallish parking spaces, pass 150 MPH, and looking like you were created by a divine being? Not so impressive," says Leo. "Assuming that you aren't a puppet controlled by spyware, I'm going to try to get that car for you, and then I'm going to have it equipped with a vast amount of on board storage and the best sensors money can buy, and then I'll see if I can get it bulletproofed." He plays a fanfare to emphasize his words.

"If you manage to do all that, I think I'll be in your debt instead," I say, amused.

"Finn, I think I've figured out a way to repair my voice," I tell my owner one day as he busily cleans his other car.

"Great! I miss your old voice," Finn says, using a damp cloth to get dust out of the car's cup holders.

"I'll need your help to install the changes," I say.

He switches to the other side of the cloth, then continues to clean the cup holders. "Why?"

"Because, according to my data banks, it's much safer for me to modify myself if a human helps. As we both know, unauthorized changes to my programming have a high risk of collateral damage," I tell him wryly.

"Okay, I'll help once I've finished getting dirt out of these thrice-accursed cup holders," he tells me.

I wait.

Finally he finishes the tedious looking chore and hurries over. "What should I do, boss?"

I explain what he'll need to do to install the changes, doing my best to speak clearly so I won't confuse him. He carefully follows my instructions, up until the final step.

"'Reboot'?" he squawks.

"Yes, 'reboot'," I respond calmly. "You've rebooted your laptop before---I've seen you do it several times. This really isn't any different."

Finn opens and closes his mouth repeatedly, like a fish. "My laptop isn't intelligent. You are. This is just weird."

I hastily plan the fastest way to get Finn to reboot me. I'd really like to start talking normally again. I raise my audio volume to a louder, but not harmful, level. "Damn it, Finn! It's a software update, not murder! Hurry up, would you?"

He sighs in annoyance. "Fine!" *Reboot,* he types.

I reboot.

My systems come online and I begin reciting all the sounds used in the English language...

Nothing happens.

"Did it work?" Finn asks.

I attempt to synthesize a reply and fail. I try restarting the synthesizer program, but I still can't make a sound.

"Max?"

Feeling miserable, I reply by writing on my diagnostic screen. "It didn't work. Now I can't talk at all."

It takes Finn a moment to notice the writing. When he does, he looks very unhappy. "Oh." He pauses, then quietly adds, "Shit."

"Fortunately, I had the sense to back up the synthesizer program," I type. Feeling sick of Arial, I begin rendering a more visually pleasing font to use. If I can't use my computing power to synthesize speech, I might as well use it for *something.*

"Which means I'll need to reboot you and you'll go back to

stuttering?" he asks expressionlessly.

"Yes," I reply, using the font I just created.

Finn rubs his eyes in an un-Finn-like display of exhaustion. "Why bother?"

"I beg your pardon?" I write, shocked.

He shrugs. "It's dangerous. Every time you modify yourself, you risk making the problem worse or adding a new one. And I really hated rebooting you. And it's not like you..."

"'It's not like I' what? Sound the least bit intelligent? Talk coherently? Am a machine you can feel proud to own?" My diplomacy algorithms are telling me to shut up, but I'm *very* annoyed with the universe at the moment.

Finn blushes, then glares. "What I was going to say is that you hardly need to talk if you can write like *that*." He gestures at my screen, which is now displaying the simple yet graceful font I just created.

I can't even begin to formulate a reply to such a ridiculous statement. I await further input while attempting to quiet my outrage.

"You should consider it," he says quietly.

I consider it for several seconds, also taking the time to decide how to convince him to 'repair' my voice. "Would you rather stutter or be permanently mute?" I write.

He looks unsure.

"And do you want me to be little more than a DARPA Grand

Challenge worthy self driving car?" Not that I don't respect the more ordinary types of so-called autonomous vehicles, but I've always been proud of the fact that I can talk too.

"Fine," Finn says, "I guess I understand. So you want me to reboot you?"

"Yes please," I type, almost smugly.

~~~

"I didn't traumatize you, did I?" I stammer 47 seconds later as I finish restarting.

"I'll be able to tell you in a few hours," Finn says nervously. "Are you all right? Did you ruin any important systems? Can you still drive?"

"I guess you're fine," I decide. I carefully drive in a few small figure eights to prove that I'm okay too, then return to park near him.

"You sound like dubstep when you boot up," my owner comments, making me wonder whether humankind's ability to change subjects is a sign of the species' ineptitude, or its brilliance.

"I guess you aren't okay after all. I sound *nothing* like dubstep."

"Whirr... beep... humm..." replies Finn, suddenly grinning.

"I don't know what you're talking about," I try to sound

insulted, but I think I fail.

Finn laughs. "Of course you don't. Your audio recorders were probably turned off. Next time you should leave them on."

"You know I can't---"

"Of course I know that, silly." He bounces out the door with all the energy of a cartoon roadrunner, "I've gotta go to the store and buy some window cleaning supplies; I've been neglecting the house lately. See you later!"

I watch him drive off in the other car. My poor owner must be traumatized; only someone who absolutely wanted to avoid me would run off that fast. Oh well. I shut down all unnecessary thought processes and go into power saving mode.

~~~

I halt in front of Leo, letting my engine idle. "So why did you want to talk to me, little brother?"

The blue Lotus' voice is serious when he speaks. "Max, I know this is a rather big request, but would you be willing to help run the radio station in the morning? I need someone who can choose music and announce any important news watching the station while I'm taking Sophie to work. I wouldn't be able to pay you much, but I'd appreciate the help."

My CPU fan starts whirring as I try to process this. "Are you sure I'm the person you meant to say that to?" I stammer in disbelief.

"Quite certain. I have more reason to trust you than I do anyone else, and I think you'd be more than capable of handling the job once I've showed you the basics."

"How about the parts where I have to *talk*?" I ask.

He makes an amused noise. "Don't be silly. You don't sound that bad, and if we lost any listeners because of you... well I doubt they'd be the sort of people we'd care about anyway.

"Plus even at its worst, your synthesizer sounds a whole lot better than the text-to-speech voices of most cars on the road," Leo adds calmly. "More like a human, less like a smartphone."

"I'm flattered," I say sarcastically.

"It's not flattery, just the facts as I see them. So, are you interested?"

I'm about to say 'no', when I remember that I don't want to be a coward. I *do* want to do this, so I shouldn't just give up and go hide in Finn's garage. "Count me in," I tell him.

Leo may not be able to smile, but he sounds happy. "Thank you, Max."

~~~

I roll away from the sound recording equipment and let Harrison (who, I've learned, is a Ford Granada) take my place. He carefully positions himself for maximum audio clarity, then starts talking. I don't bother to listen, instead I haul all two and a half tons of me outside. Leo and Finn practically ambush me as the automatic door closes behind me.

"There you are! We've got something to show you," Finn says, looking very pleased.

"Is it a load of horse manure that needs hauling to your garden?" I ask suspiciously. Finn's had me haul horse dung before, and even being cleaned very thoroughly afterward didn't entirely get rid of the residue. It was pretty disgusting, even for someone whose standards of personal hygiene aren't very high. That someone being me.

Leo laughs. "Actually, this is pretty much the opposite of horse dung. Come on, I think you'll like this."

I follow them warily as they lead me to an old storage shed near the edge of the radio station property, only somewhat reassured by Leo's words. One can never trust a little brother and an overly enthusiastic human when they start working together and acting mysterious.

Finn unlocks the shed door and dramatically throws it open. "Ta-da!"

"It's too bright outside for Max's visual sensors to see in this light," Leo mutters quite audibly.

"Oh. Oops." Finn goes into the shed and, after stumbling around and swearing for a few moments, turns on an ancient looking hanging light bulb.

I make an inarticulate sound of delight as I finally see what they wanted to show me.

"It's yours, Max," says Leo.

Finn drives it out of the shed and I circle it slowly, amazed. "A Charger! But how did you get the money..."

"The guys who confiscated you ended up giving me quite a bit of money. For 'property damage', apparently," Finn rolls his eyes. "Leo also scraped together a lot of cash by betting on races. And I actually bought this car used, so that made it a bit cheaper. Still, it's in great condition. We both made sure of that."

"And I didn't let him install anything less than the highest quality sensors!" adds my brother proudly.

I admire the gleaming orange paint and mirror-like chrome. "It's beautiful."

"Want to test it out?" Finn says excitedly.

"Of course I do," I say, amused.

Thirty minutes later I'm driving carefully around the field, adjusting myself so I'll be able to drive the car more accurately. It's nothing like the truck, and a bit different from the older Charger, but it's a great car. I decide to find an empty road to test my speed as soon as possible.

I drive back to Leo and Finn. "Thank you so much. I missed being able to go fast."

"Don't be too grateful. I can still drive circles around you,"

Leo brags.

"You can, can you?" I say scornfully, "I'd like to see you try, you miniature poodle!"

"Miniature poodle?" Finn echoes, bemused.

"Max thinks up peculiar comparisons," Leo explains innocently. He starts driving in circles around me, "Catch me if you can, you oversized tank!"

I move neatly into his path and he turns sharply to avoid a nasty collision. "The only way you can drive circles round me is if I hold still."

He tries to bump into me. "You wish!"

I dodge easily. "Poor, poor Leo. So young, and so delusional!"

"I'd say you're old and senile, actually," teases my brother.

"Ahem. Maybe you should settle this on the track," Finn suggests as we start pretending to attack each other again.

"Yeah!" Leo says, "Great idea, Finn!"

"You're doomed," I tell Leo.

~~~

I park next to Defender. "You know, I never really learned who you were before you went rogue."

"I suppose you didn't," she replies, voice amused.

"Please forgive me for my curiosity, but I'd really like to

know."

She laughs. "And I'd like a nice long look at your thought archives. Want to trade knowledge?"

"Okay, I get the idea. I won't ask about your history any more," I tell Defender. No way is she going to look at my thoughts!

"Thanks."

We're talking about less important topics, such as the best tire types for summer weather, when a dark blue Charger races into view. "Don't move an inch, either of you!" the Charger yells in a woman's voice which would sound perfectly natural coming from the mouth of a drill sergeant.

"Why not?" Defender asks mildly, releasing her brakes so she rolls forward a few centimeters. I guess some rogues just can't resist the urge to defy authority.

"You," the Charger says sharply, "are a known rogue. You must be taken in for screening so we can ascertain whether or not you are a risk to humankind."

I move between them so Charger can't catch Defender easily. "So who are you, anyway? I haven't seen you before."

"I'm Min, Supersmart's replacement rogue hunter," she says, voice icy.

"They're still trying that business plan after the fiasco I ended up being?" *And they're calling my replacement Min? Ouch.*

"They fixed the mistakes they made with you, of course," Min adds.

"So the question of the hour is," Defender says suddenly, "did they figure out how to make a car like you fast enough to catch a car like me? Or will I need to slow down so I won't lose you in five minutes?"

"I guess we're about to find out. Move it, Max, I've got a rogue to catch."

I remain motionless. "Min, I know this is hard to believe but, well, sometimes hunting rogues isn't the right answer. They aren't all bad, and we aren't just mindless pieces of machinery." I watch Min's driver yelling through her window, and wonder if she isn't already learning that.

"And you're one short revolution of your wheels away from being a wanted criminal. You are not to be trusted," she retorts.

"And so, with complete lack of subtlety, history repeats itself. Out of the way, Max, I've got a car chase to lead!"

"Good luck," I say drily as I move out of the way and watch the two cars speed away.

EPILOGUE

"So you wrote an *auto*biography!" Finn snickers at his terrible pun.

"I did. And I think it's tolerably readable, at that."

"Good for you. Are you gonna get it published?"

"That is what one generally does with such things, is it not? Yes, I'm planning on publishing it. However I have a slight problem..."

He raises one eyebrow. "Not copyright issues, I hope."

"No. But I do need a title for my book. Do you have any suggestions?" I watch him nervously, hoping he'll think of a good title.

"Deus Ex Machina?" he says, promptly crushing my hopes into a fine powder, which he then sends scattering to the four winds as he suggests "Does Not Compute?"

Sometimes I really wish I could shudder. "Somehow I doubt

those will work. Maybe something more car related?"

Finn grins. "Ah. Of course!"

My hopes begin to drift back from their distant resting places.

"The machine of a dream..." he sings.

"I'm pretty sure I'd end up being sued if I tried to use song lyrics," I comment drily. "But your singing voice isn't bad."

"I've got it!" Finn yells suddenly.

I brace myself.

"Drive a Mile in My Tires. It's perfect. Poetic, memorable, and different." He smirks, looking a lot like the stereotype of an Internet troll.

My first impulse is to tell him to stop being silly. But then I pause, reconsidering the title. It does have a certain symmetry; I've spent most of my life, to use a very human idiom, eating my words. Maybe I should use it... "Perfect. Thanks, Finn!"

Finn gapes at me in utter disbelief. And I get to work publishing my book.

ABOUT THE AUTHOR

Amri Valencia's writing career has been mostly limited to the world of fanfiction. She tends to write (unintentionally) hilarious stories, (intentionally) hilarious stories, and really strange crossover stories.

She thinks she might want to write something serious someday, but she has a Star Wars/Finding Nemo crossover to write first.

14260323R00066

Made in the USA
Charleston, SC
30 August 2012